DROUGHT DAZE

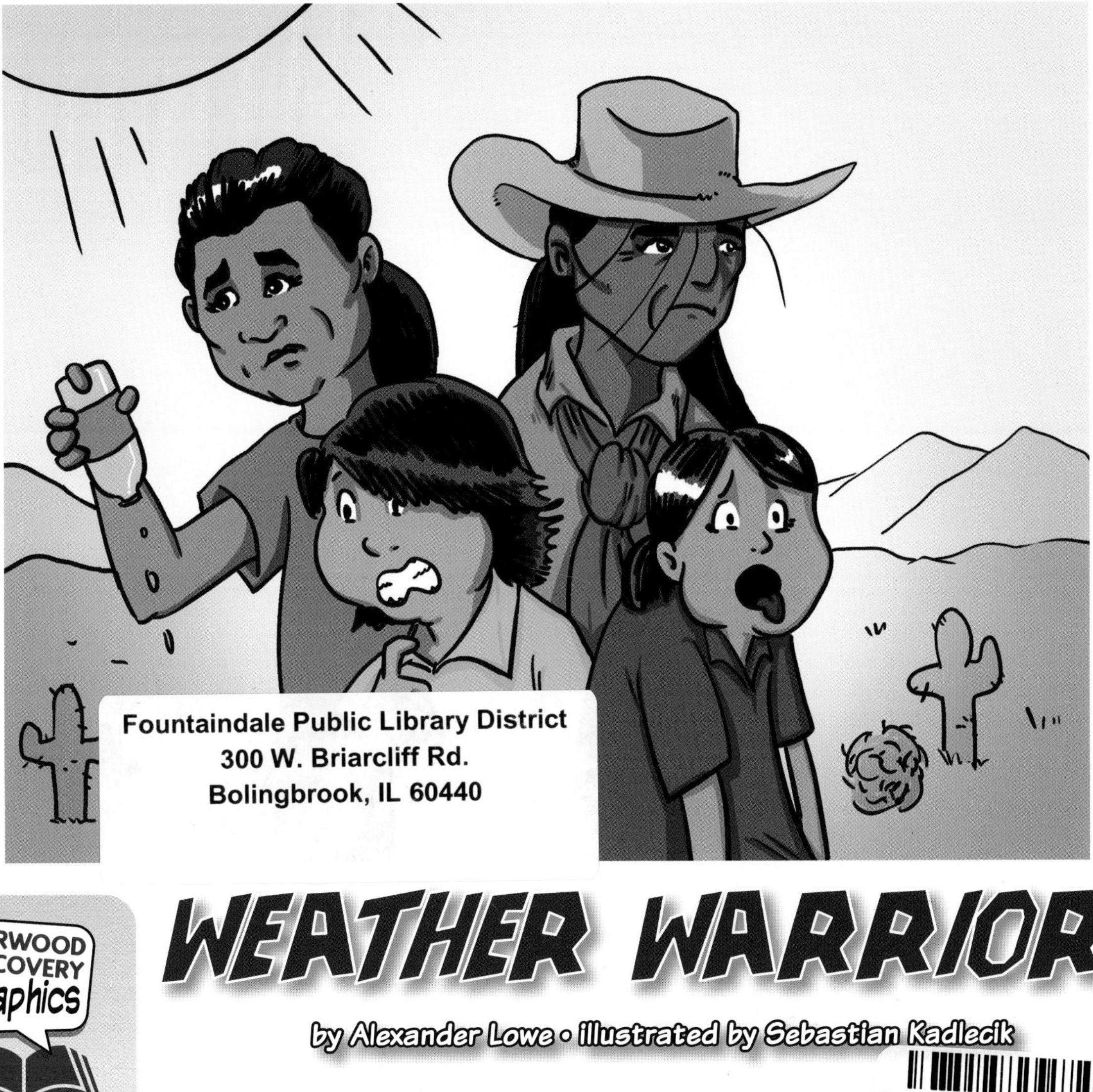

NORWOOD DISCOVERY Graphics

WEATHER WARRIORS

by Alexander Lowe • illustrated by Sebastian Kadlecik

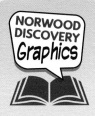

Norwood House Press

For more information about Norwood House Press please visit our website at: www.norwoodhousepress.com or call 866-565-2900.

Library of Congress Cataloging-in-Publication Data
Names: Lowe, Alexander, author. | Kadlecik, Sebastian, illustrator.
Title: Drought daze / by Alexander Lowe ; illustrated by Sebastian Kadlecik.
Description: Chicago : Norwood House Press, [2021] | Series: Norwood discovery graphics | Audience: Ages 8-10 | Audience: Grades
    4-6 | Summary: "Follow a family as they visit an aunt on her drought-stricken ranch in Central California. An adventure-filled
    graphic novel that provides young readers information about droughts and severe dry conditions. Learn from these weather
    warriors how droughts affect people, how they must adapt, how to conserve, and how to prevent fires during a drought. Includes
    contemporary full-color graphic artwork, fun facts, additional information, and a glossary"— Provided by publisher.
Identifiers: LCCN 2020024508 (print) | LCCN 2020024509 (ebook) | ISBN 9781684508563 (hardcover)
    | ISBN 9781684045914 (paperback) | ISBN 9781684045969 (epub)
Subjects: LCSH: Droughts—Comic books, strips, etc. | Droughts—Juvenile literature. | Droughts—
    California—Juvenile literature. | Graphic novels. | CYAC: Graphic novels.
Classification: LCC QC929.27.C22 L69 2021 (print) | LCC QC929.27.C22 (ebook) | DDC 363.34/92909794—dc23
LC record available at https://lccn.loc.gov/2020024508
LC ebook record available at https://lccn.loc.gov/2020024509

Hardcover ISBN: 978-1-68450-856-3   Paperback ISBN: 978-1-68404-591-4

328N—072020
Manufactured in the United States of America in North Mankato, Minnesota.

CONTENTS

MEET THE WEATHER WARRIORS

Aunt Cassie

Mom

Ryan

Reese

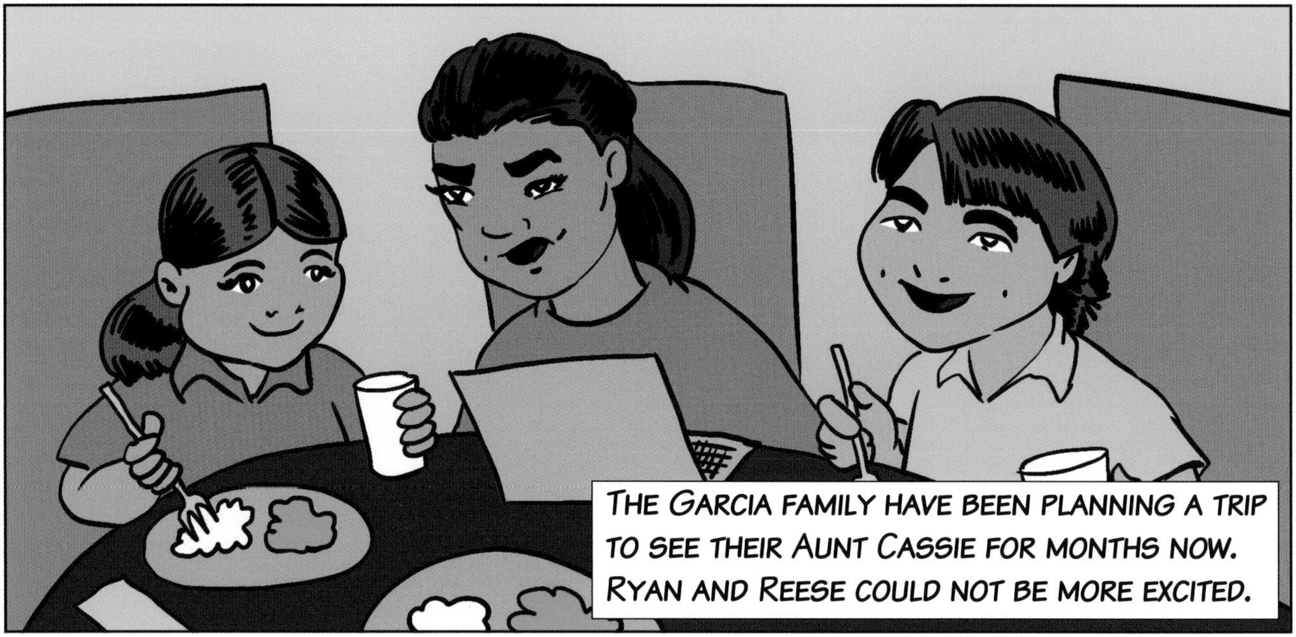
THE GARCIA FAMILY HAVE BEEN PLANNING A TRIP TO SEE THEIR AUNT CASSIE FOR MONTHS NOW. RYAN AND REESE COULD NOT BE MORE EXCITED.

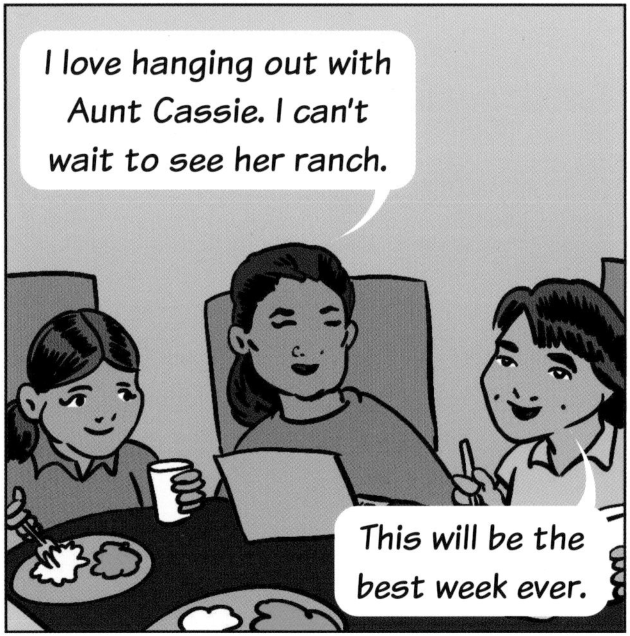
I love hanging out with Aunt Cassie. I can't wait to see her ranch.
This will be the best week ever.

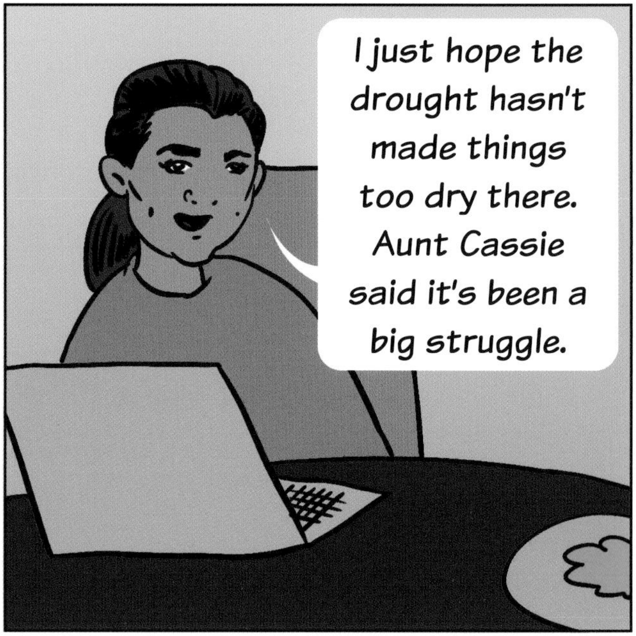
I just hope the drought hasn't made things too dry there. Aunt Cassie said it's been a big struggle.

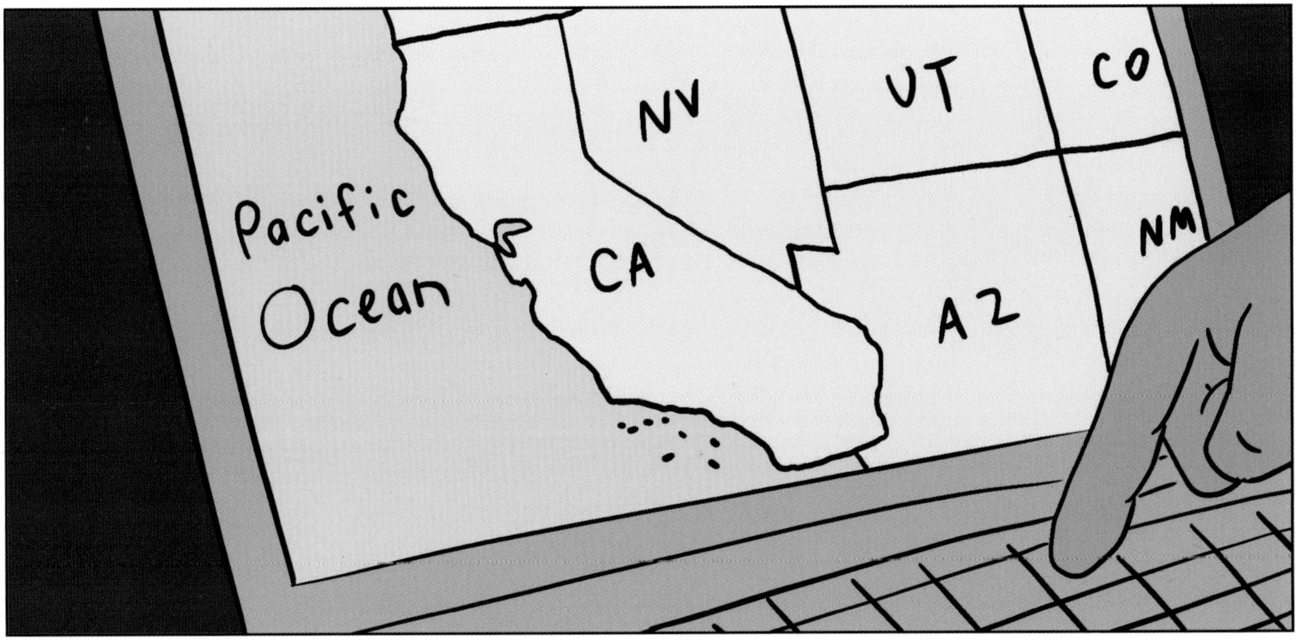

NV
UT
CO
Pacific Ocean
CA
NM
AZ

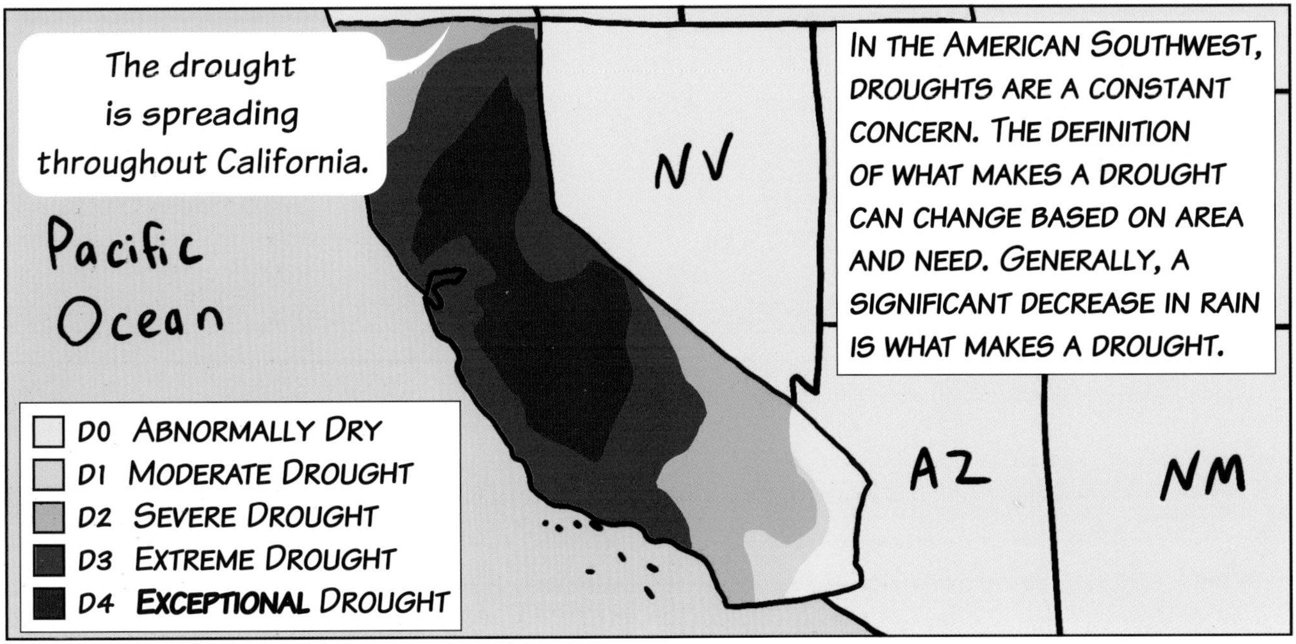

The drought is spreading throughout California.
NV
Pacific Ocean
In the American Southwest, droughts are a constant concern. The definition of what makes a drought can change based on area and need. Generally, a significant decrease in rain is what makes a drought.
AZ
NM
D0 Abnormally Dry
D1 Moderate Drought
D2 Severe Drought
D3 Extreme Drought
D4 Exceptional Drought

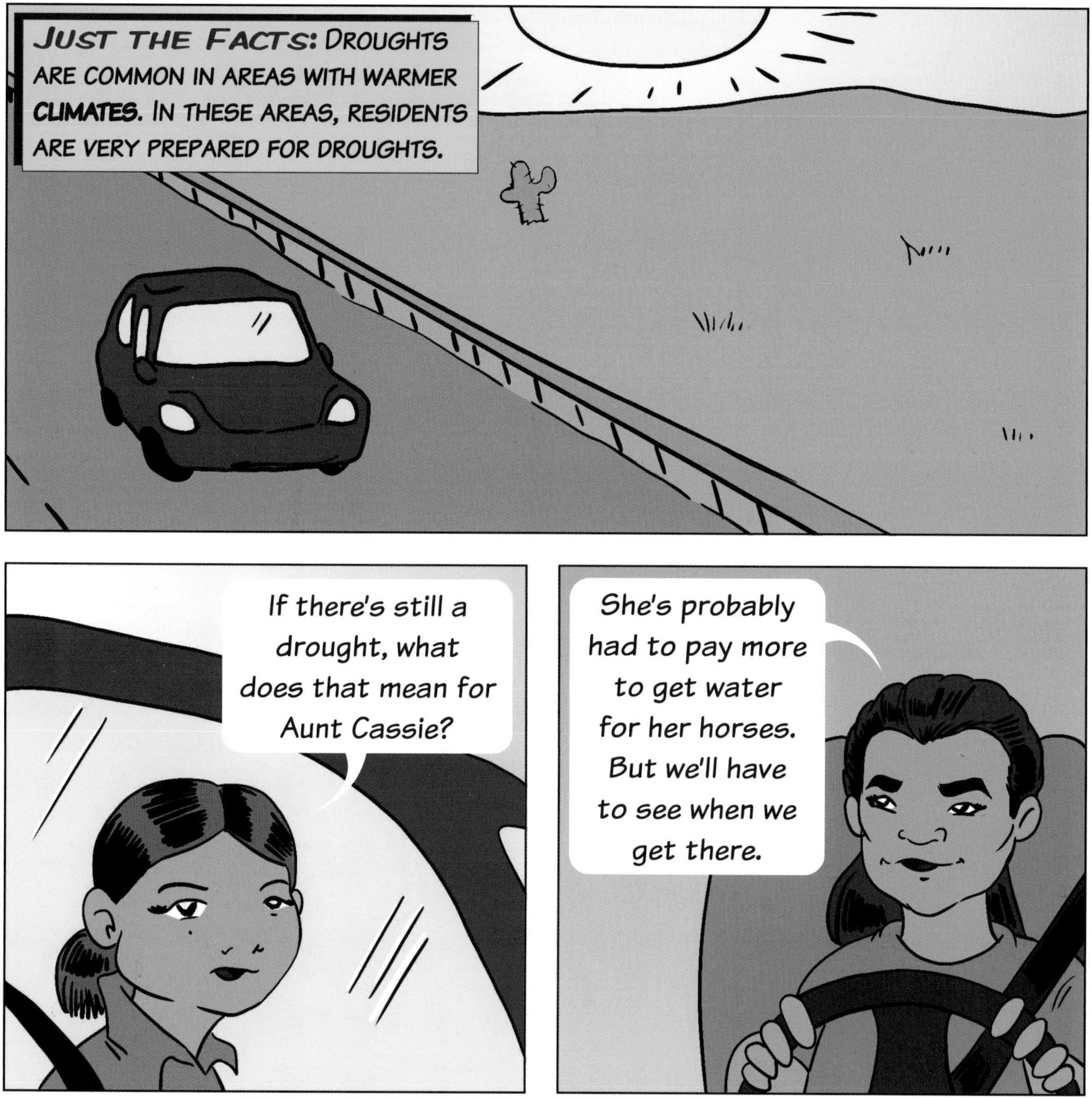
JUST THE FACTS: DROUGHTS ARE COMMON IN AREAS WITH WARMER **CLIMATES**. IN THESE AREAS, RESIDENTS ARE VERY PREPARED FOR DROUGHTS.
If there's still a drought, what does that mean for Aunt Cassie?
She's probably had to pay more to get water for her horses. But we'll have to see when we get there.

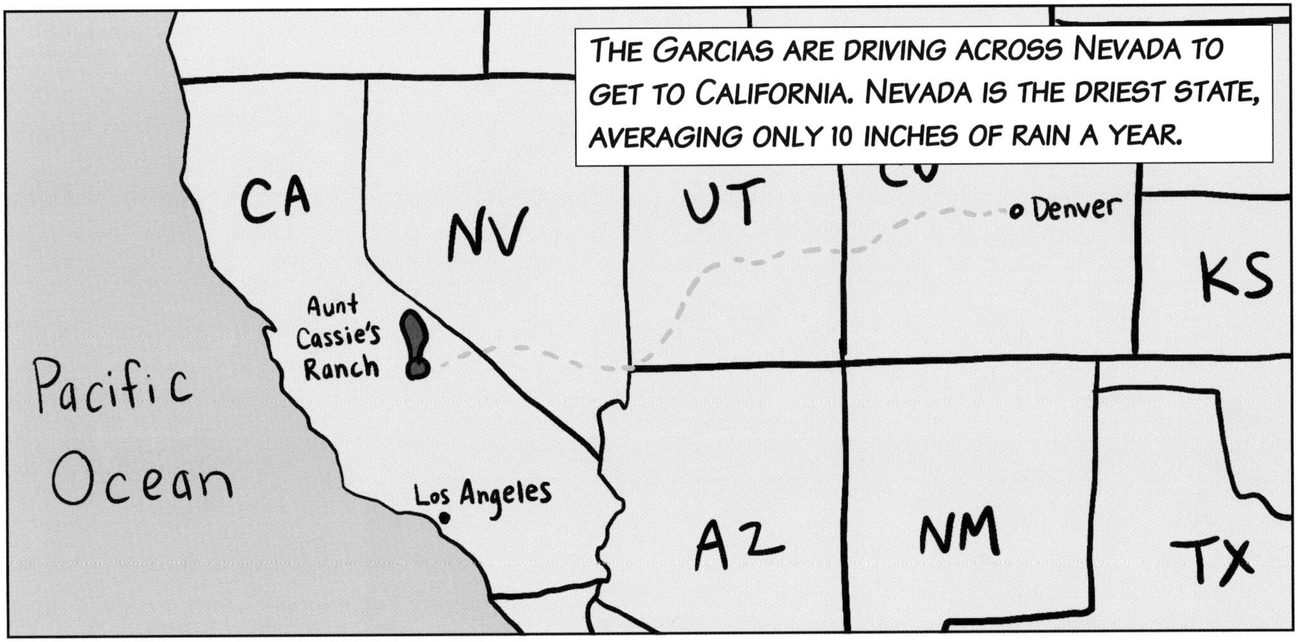
THE GARCIAS ARE DRIVING ACROSS NEVADA TO GET TO CALIFORNIA. NEVADA IS THE DRIEST STATE, AVERAGING ONLY 10 INCHES OF RAIN A YEAR.
CA
NV
UT
Denver
KS
Aunt Cassie's Ranch
Pacific Ocean
Los Angeles
AZ
NM
TX

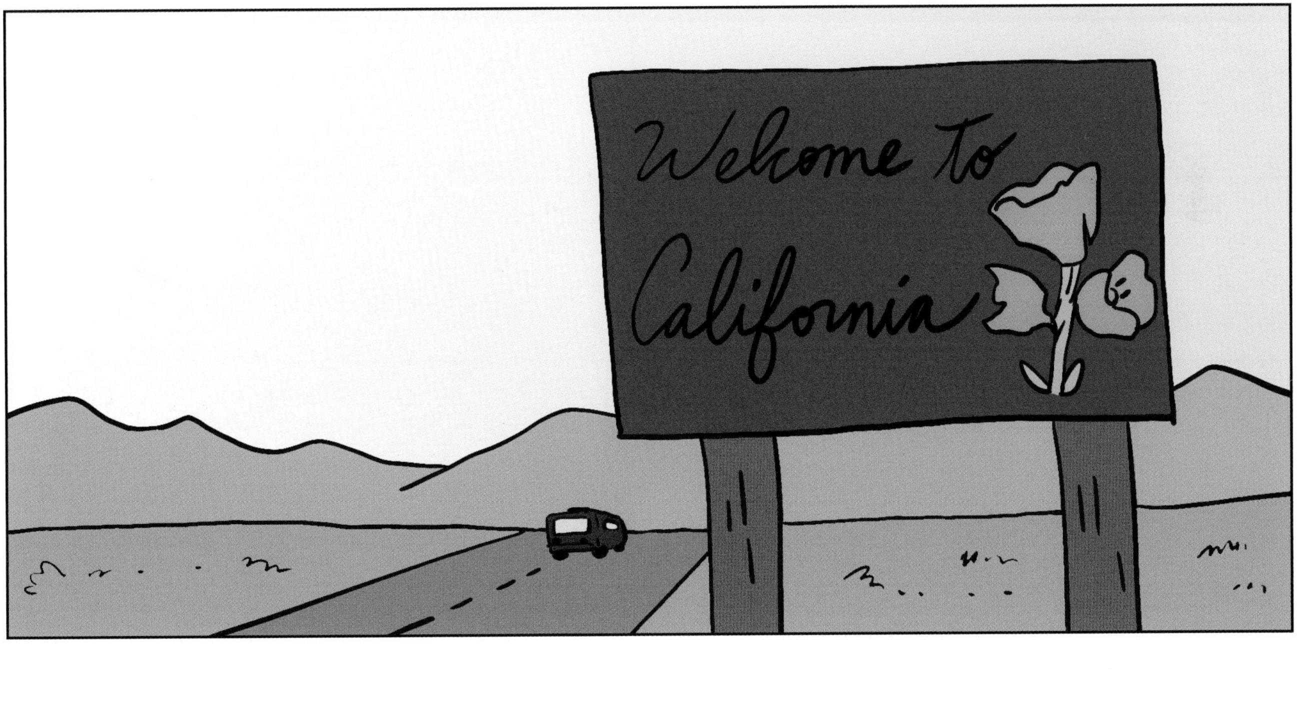
Welcome to California

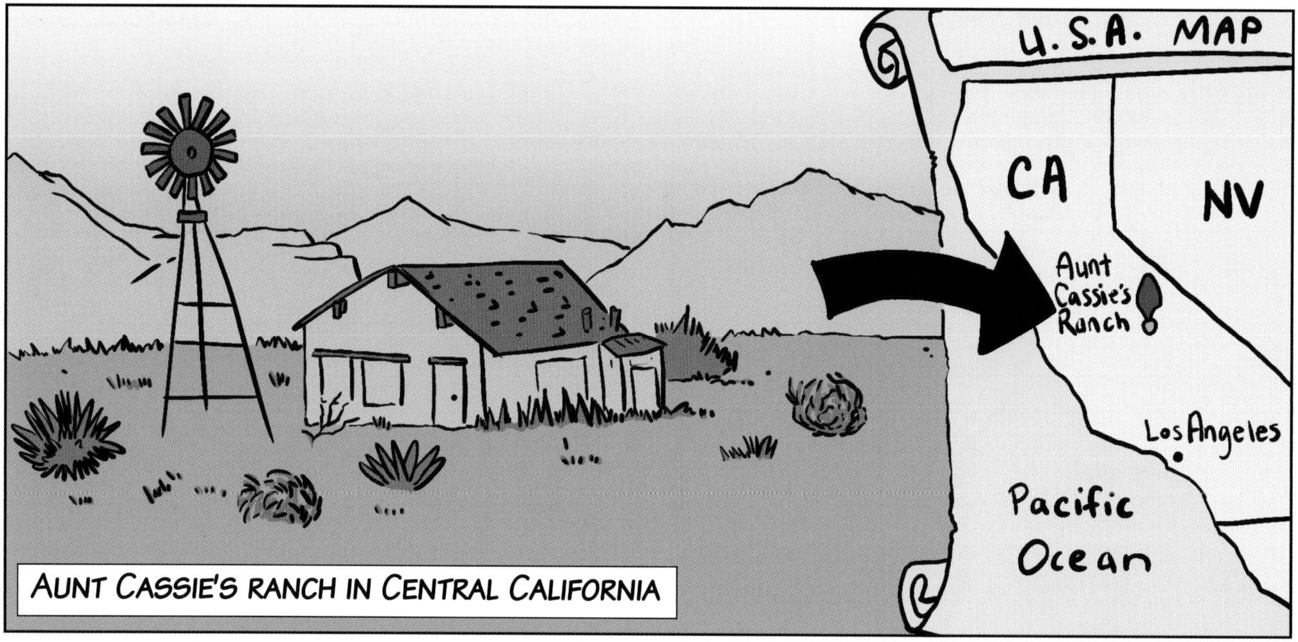
U.S.A. MAP
CA
NV
Aunt Cassie's Ranch
Los Angeles
Pacific Ocean
AUNT CASSIE'S RANCH IN CENTRAL CALIFORNIA

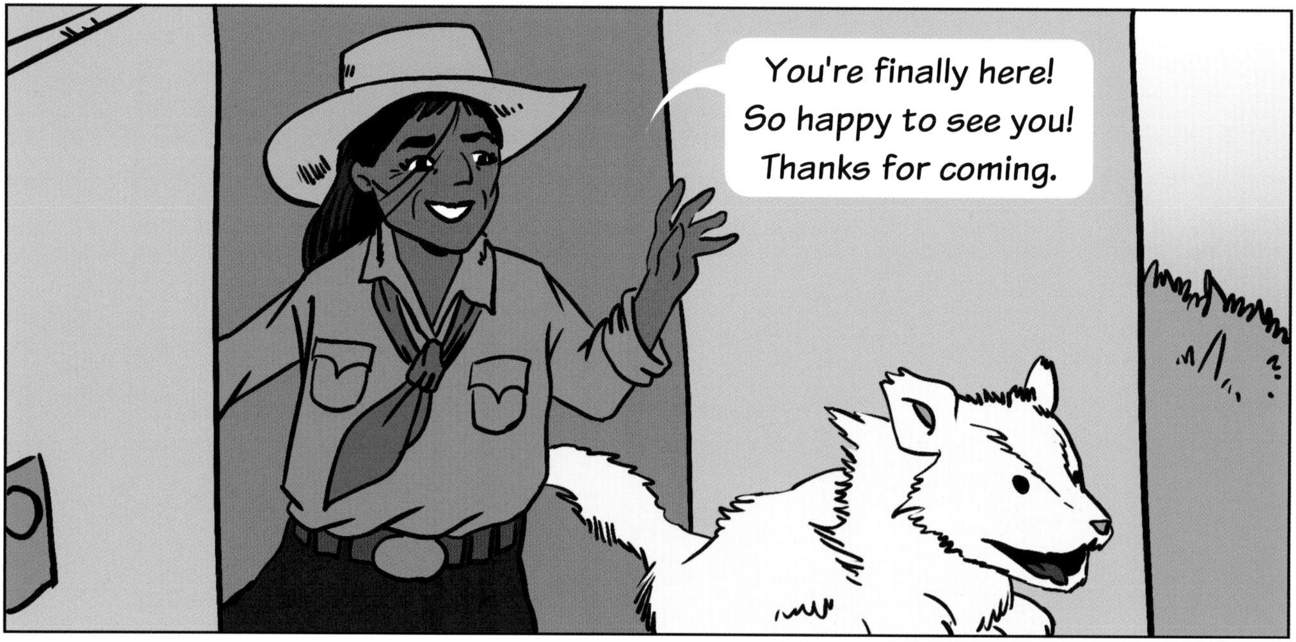
You're finally here! So happy to see you! Thanks for coming.

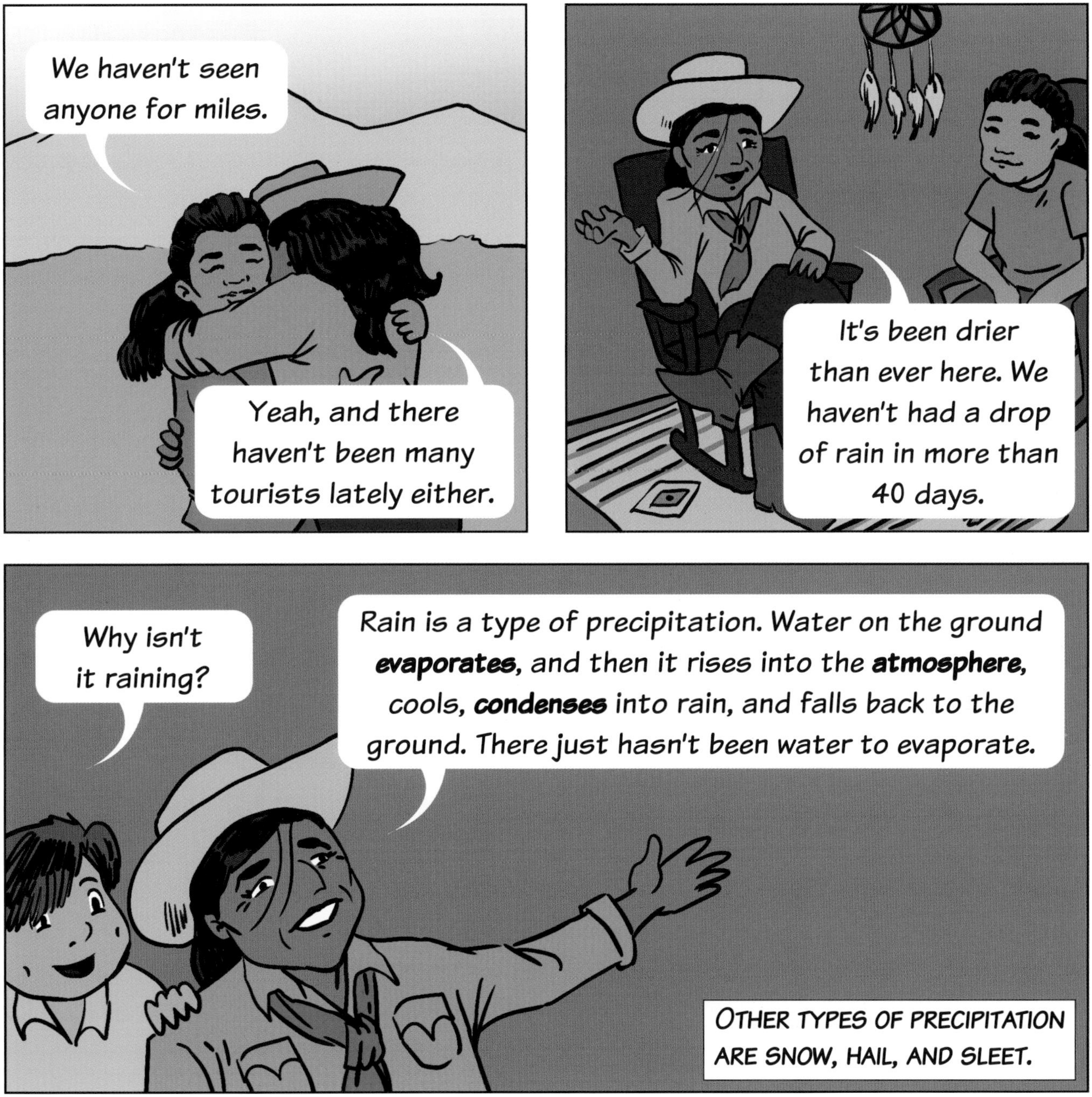
We haven't seen anyone for miles.
Yeah, and there haven't been many tourists lately either.
It's been drier than ever here. We haven't had a drop of rain in more than 40 days.
Why isn't it raining?
Rain is a type of precipitation. Water on the ground **evaporates**, and then it rises into the **atmosphere**, cools, **condenses** into rain, and falls back to the ground. There just hasn't been water to evaporate.
OTHER TYPES OF PRECIPITATION ARE SNOW, HAIL, AND SLEET.

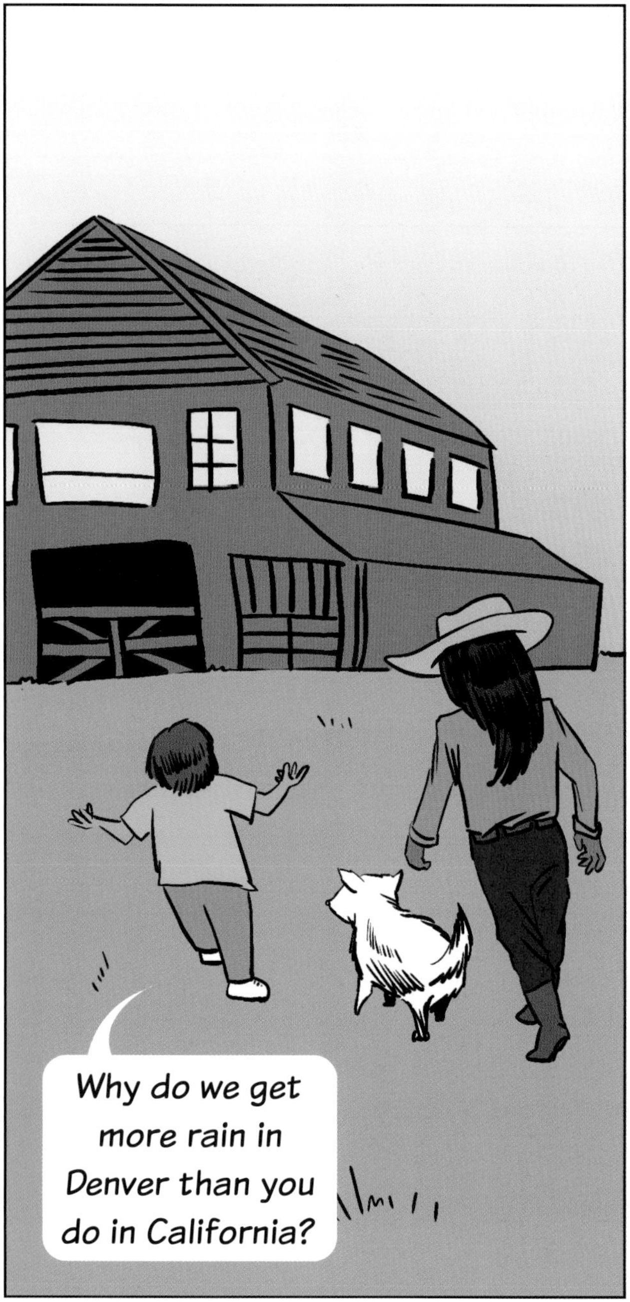
Why do we get more rain in Denver than you do in California?

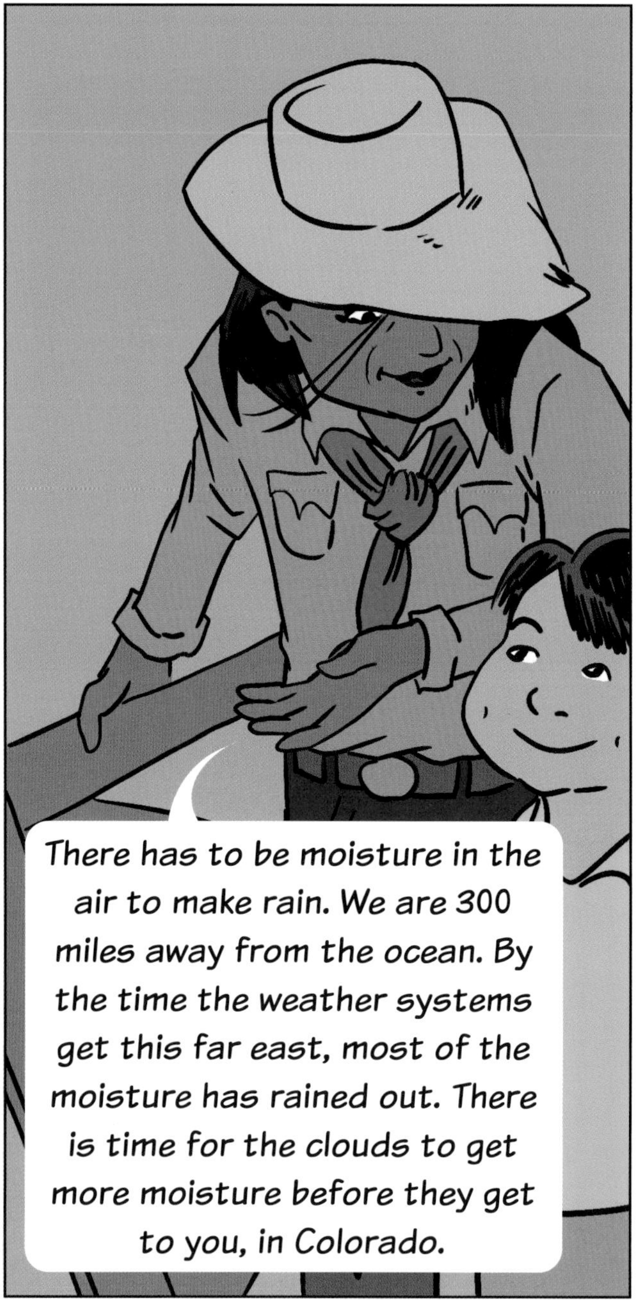
There has to be moisture in the air to make rain. We are 300 miles away from the ocean. By the time the weather systems get this far east, most of the moisture has rained out. There is time for the clouds to get more moisture before they get to you, in Colorado.

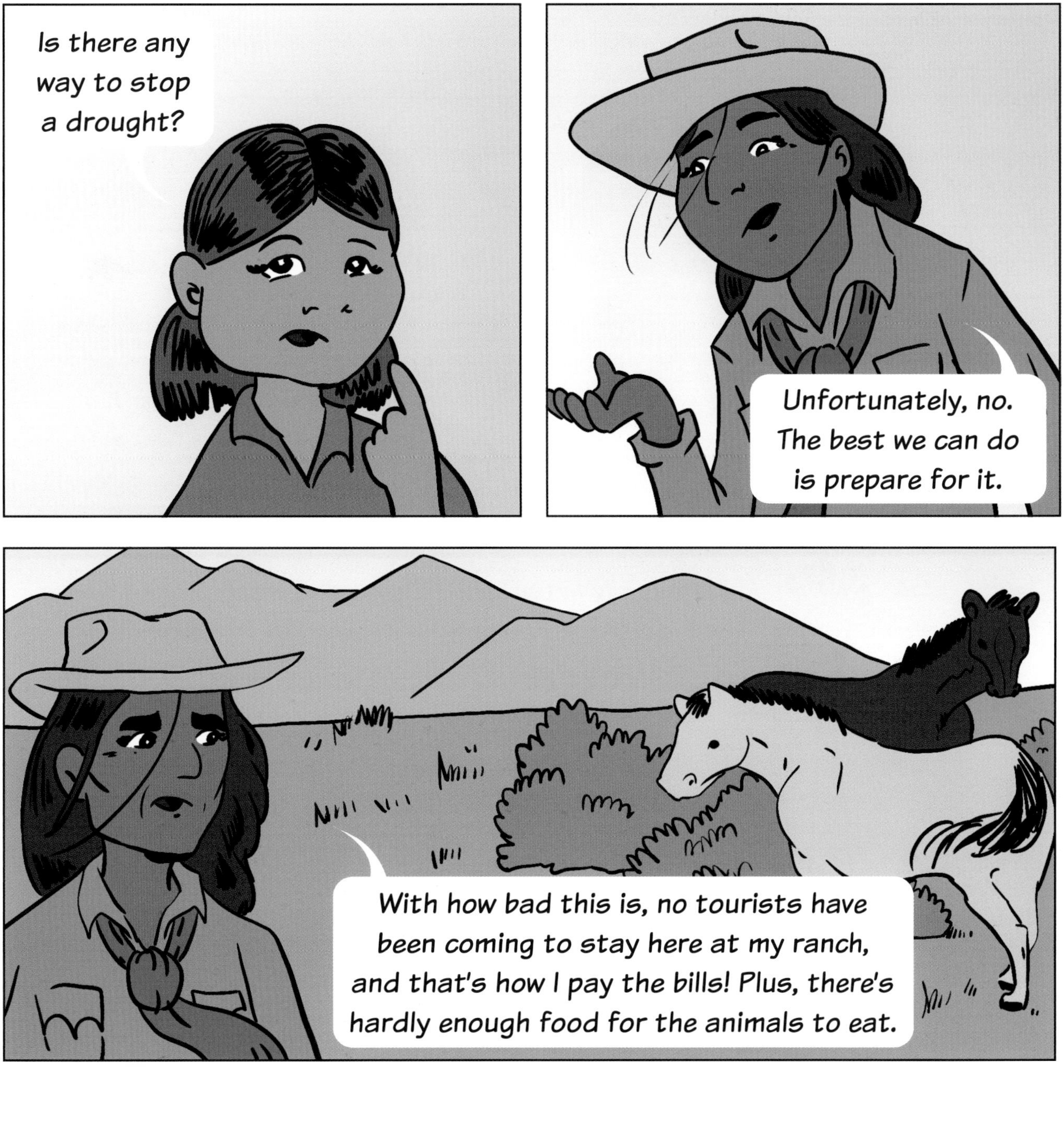
Is there any way to stop a drought?
Unfortunately, no. The best we can do is prepare for it.
With how bad this is, no tourists have been coming to stay here at my ranch, and that's how I pay the bills! Plus, there's hardly enough food for the animals to eat.

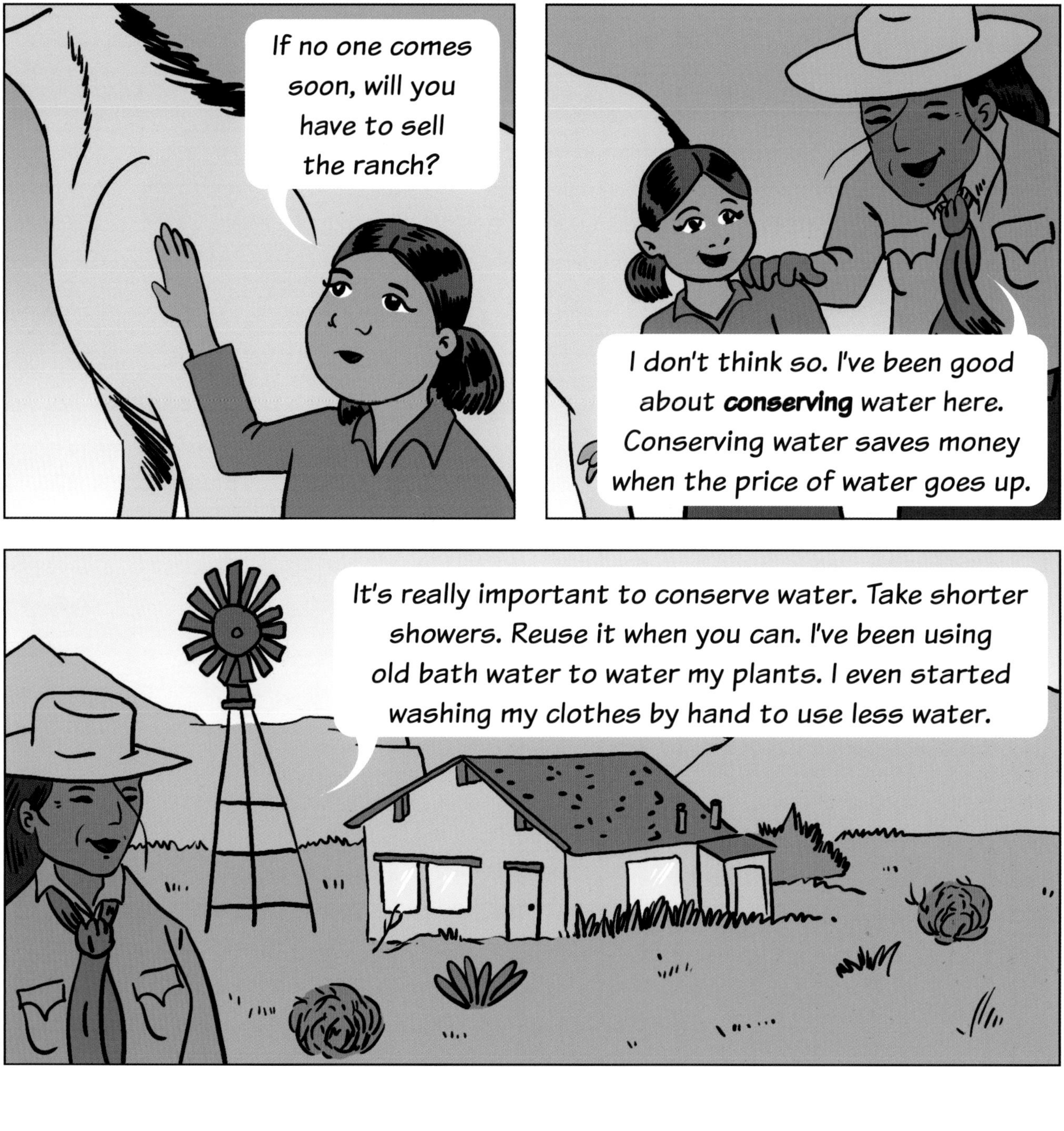
If no one comes soon, will you have to sell the ranch?
I don't think so. I've been good about **conserving** water here. Conserving water saves money when the price of water goes up.
It's really important to conserve water. Take shorter showers. Reuse it when you can. I've been using old bath water to water my plants. I even started washing my clothes by hand to use less water.

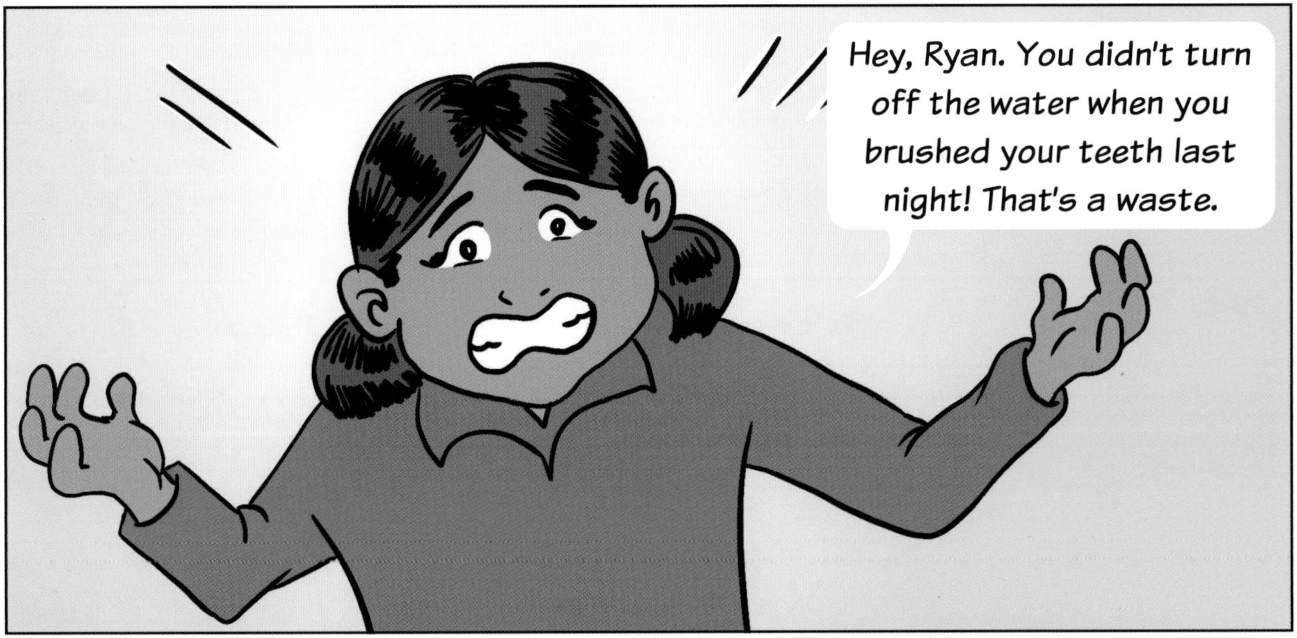
Hey, Ryan. You didn't turn off the water when you brushed your teeth last night! That's a waste.

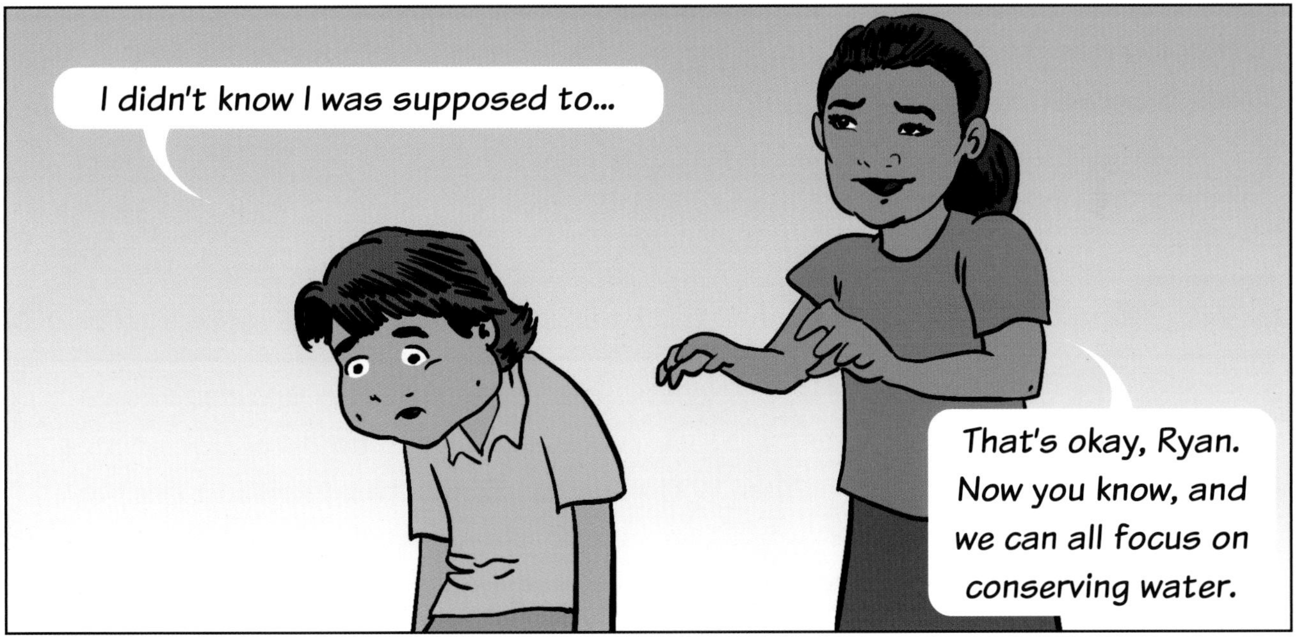
I didn't know I was supposed to...
That's okay, Ryan. Now you know, and we can all focus on conserving water.

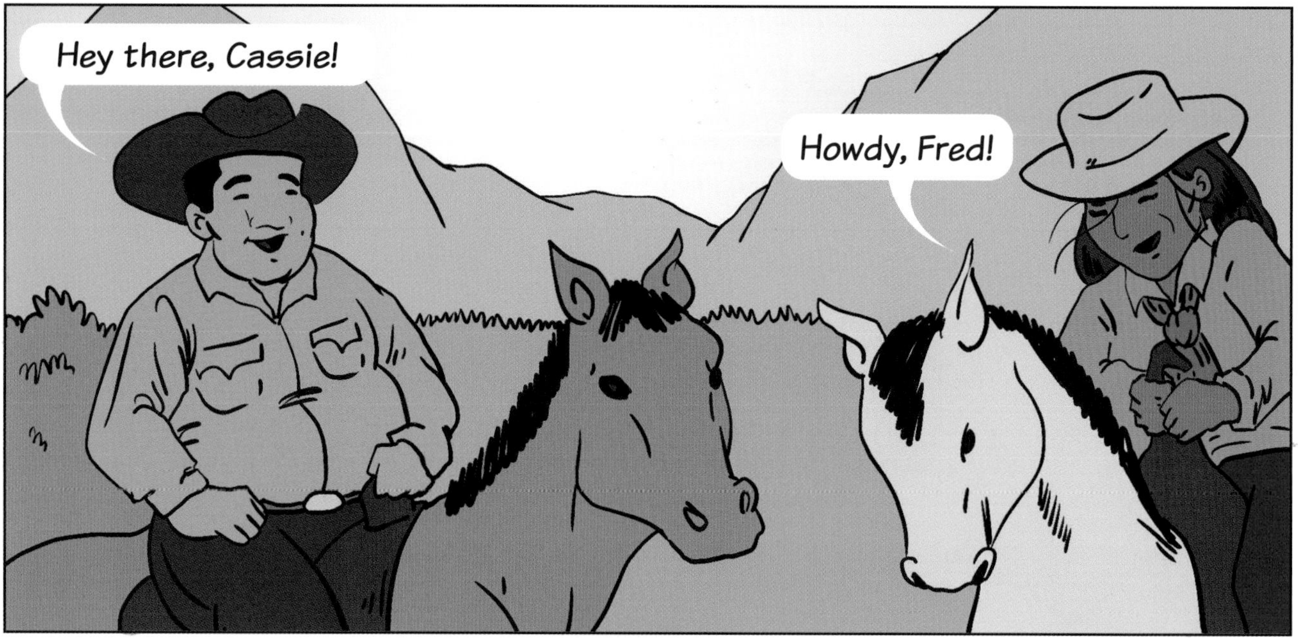
Hey there, Cassie!
Howdy, Fred!

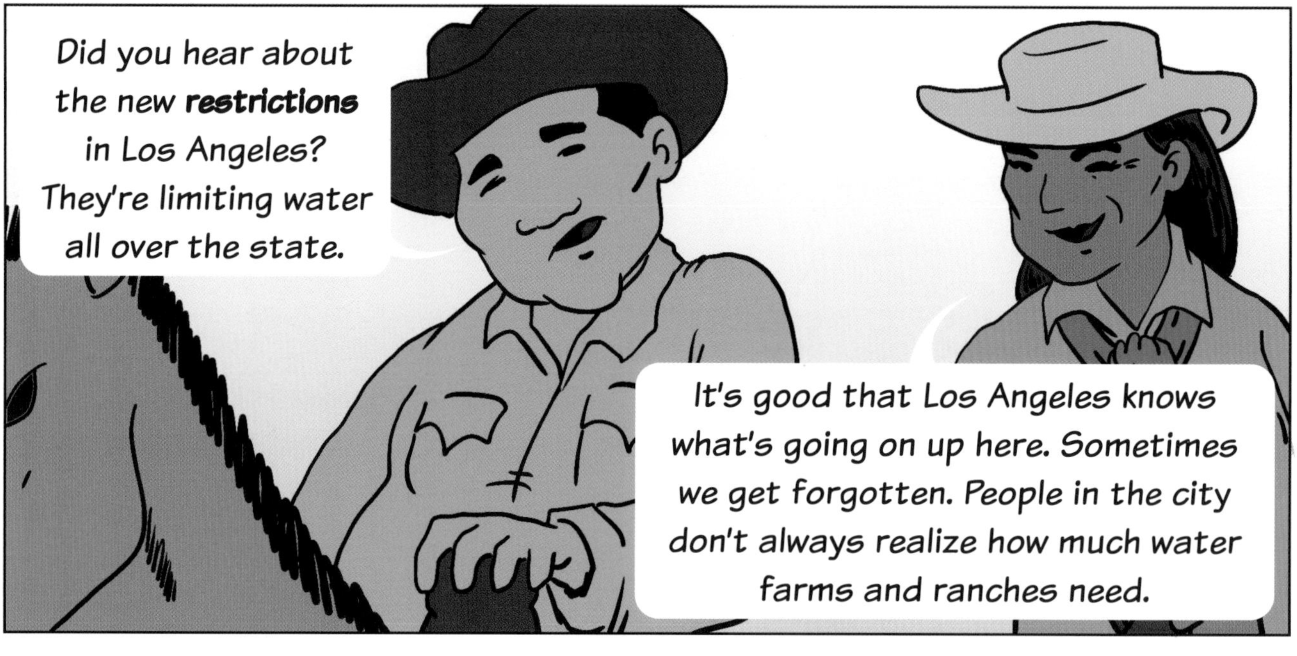
Did you hear about the new **restrictions** in Los Angeles? They're limiting water all over the state.
It's good that Los Angeles knows what's going on up here. Sometimes we get forgotten. People in the city don't always realize how much water farms and ranches need.

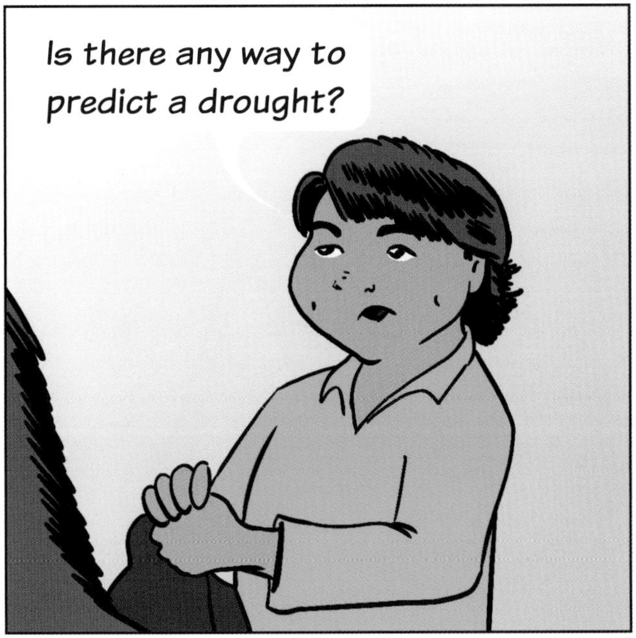
Is there any way to predict a drought?

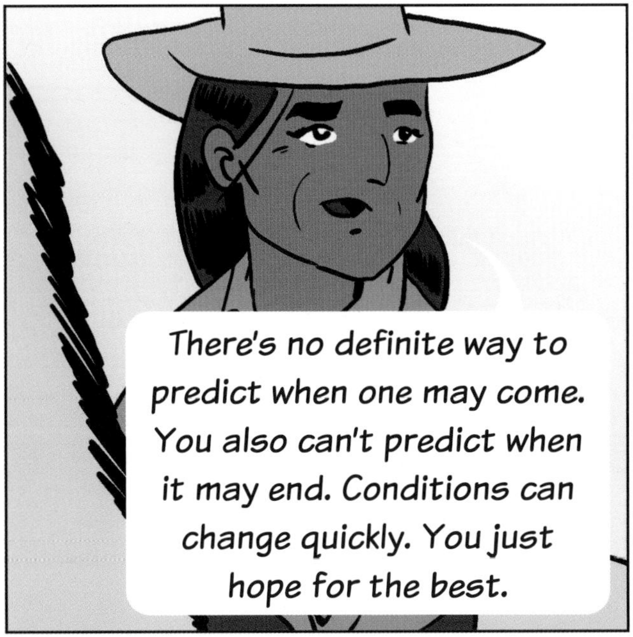
There's no definite way to predict when one may come. You also can't predict when it may end. Conditions can change quickly. You just hope for the best.

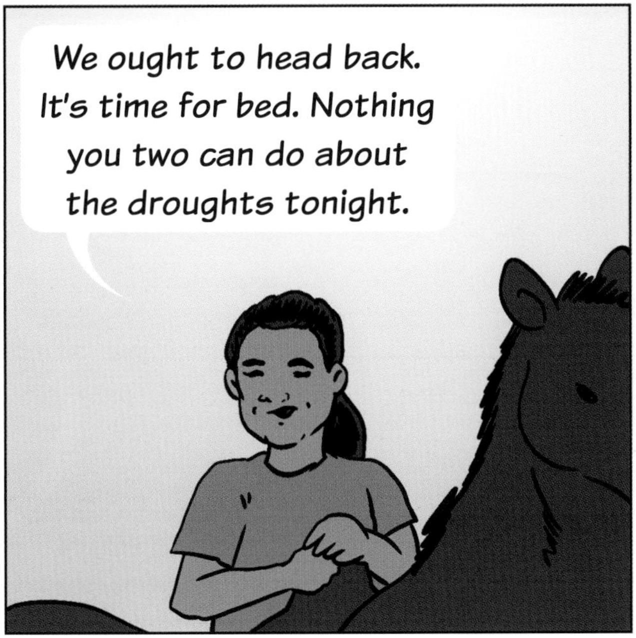
We ought to head back. It's time for bed. Nothing you two can do about the droughts tonight.

Worst Droughts in US History

The most famous drought is the Dust Bowl. It affected Texas, Oklahoma, Colorado, New Mexico, and Kansas from 1930 to 1936. Then, from 1950 to 1957, Texas rainfall was 40 percent lower than normal. In 1988, the costliest drought in US history hit the West Coast. It mostly impacted California. There were many forest fires. Damage was estimated to cost $42.4 billion.

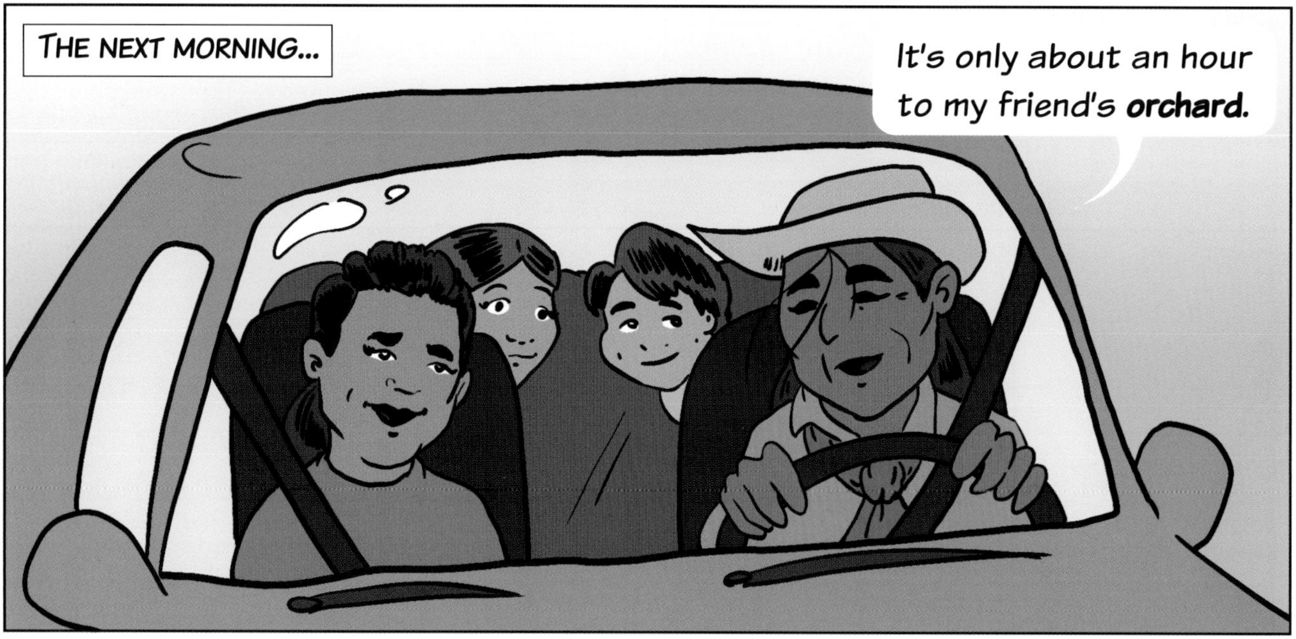
THE NEXT MORNING...
It's only about an hour to my friend's **orchard.**

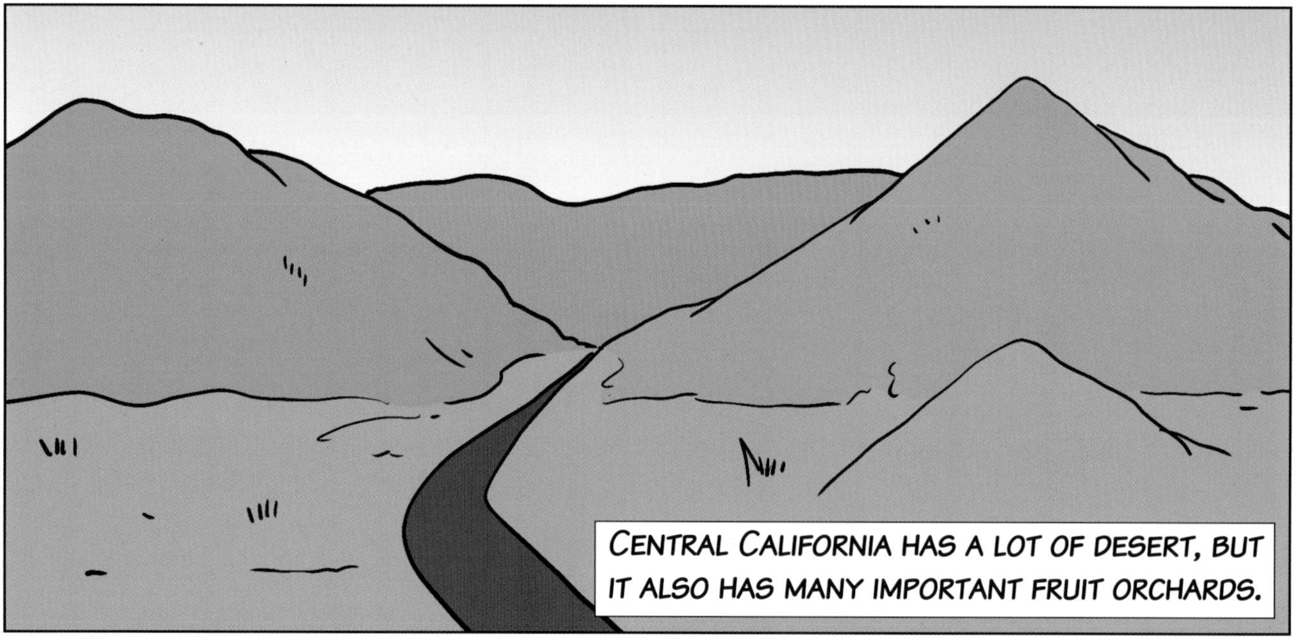
CENTRAL CALIFORNIA HAS A LOT OF DESERT, BUT IT ALSO HAS MANY IMPORTANT FRUIT ORCHARDS.

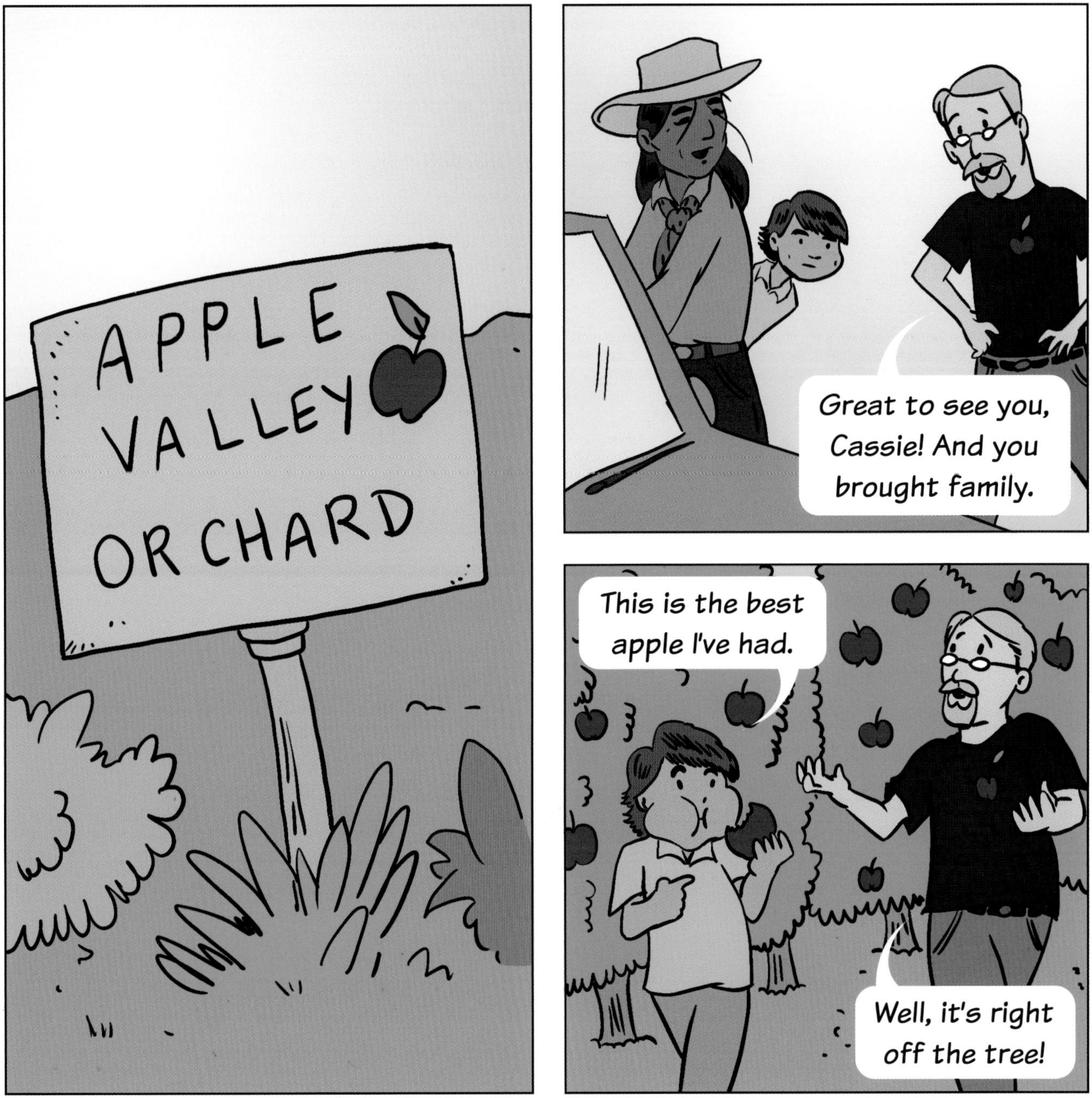
APPLE VALLEY ORCHARD
Great to see you, Cassie! And you brought family.
This is the best apple I've had.
Well, it's right off the tree!

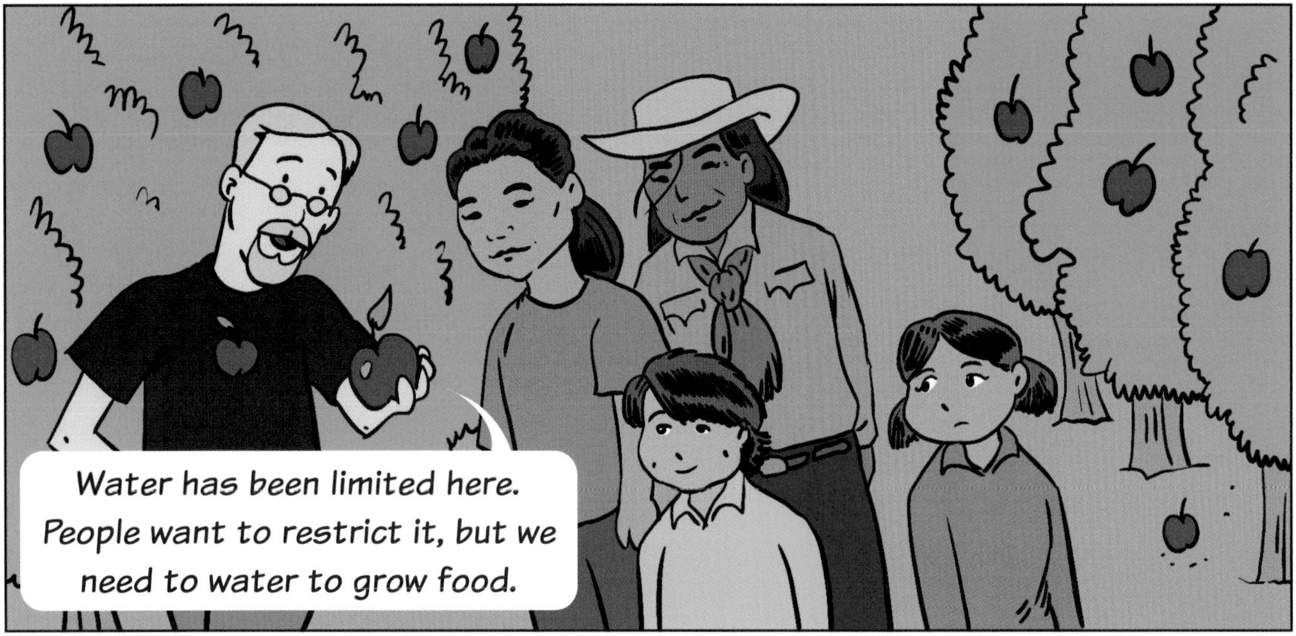
Water has been limited here. People want to restrict it, but we need to water to grow food.

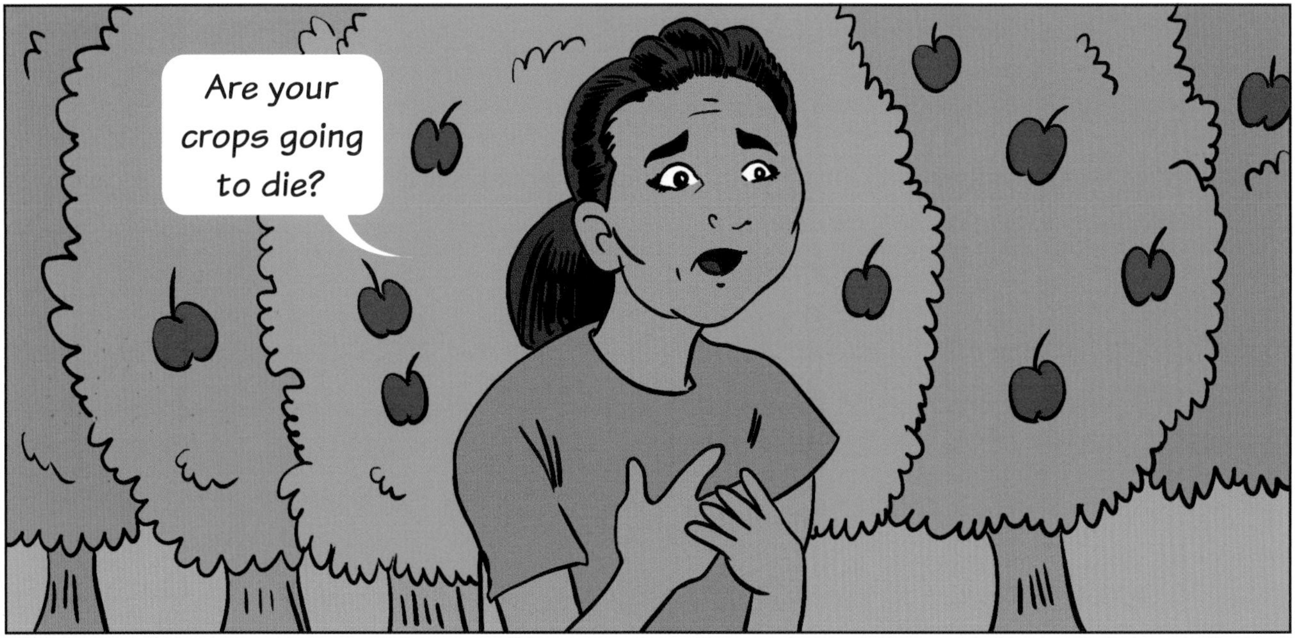
Are your crops going to die?

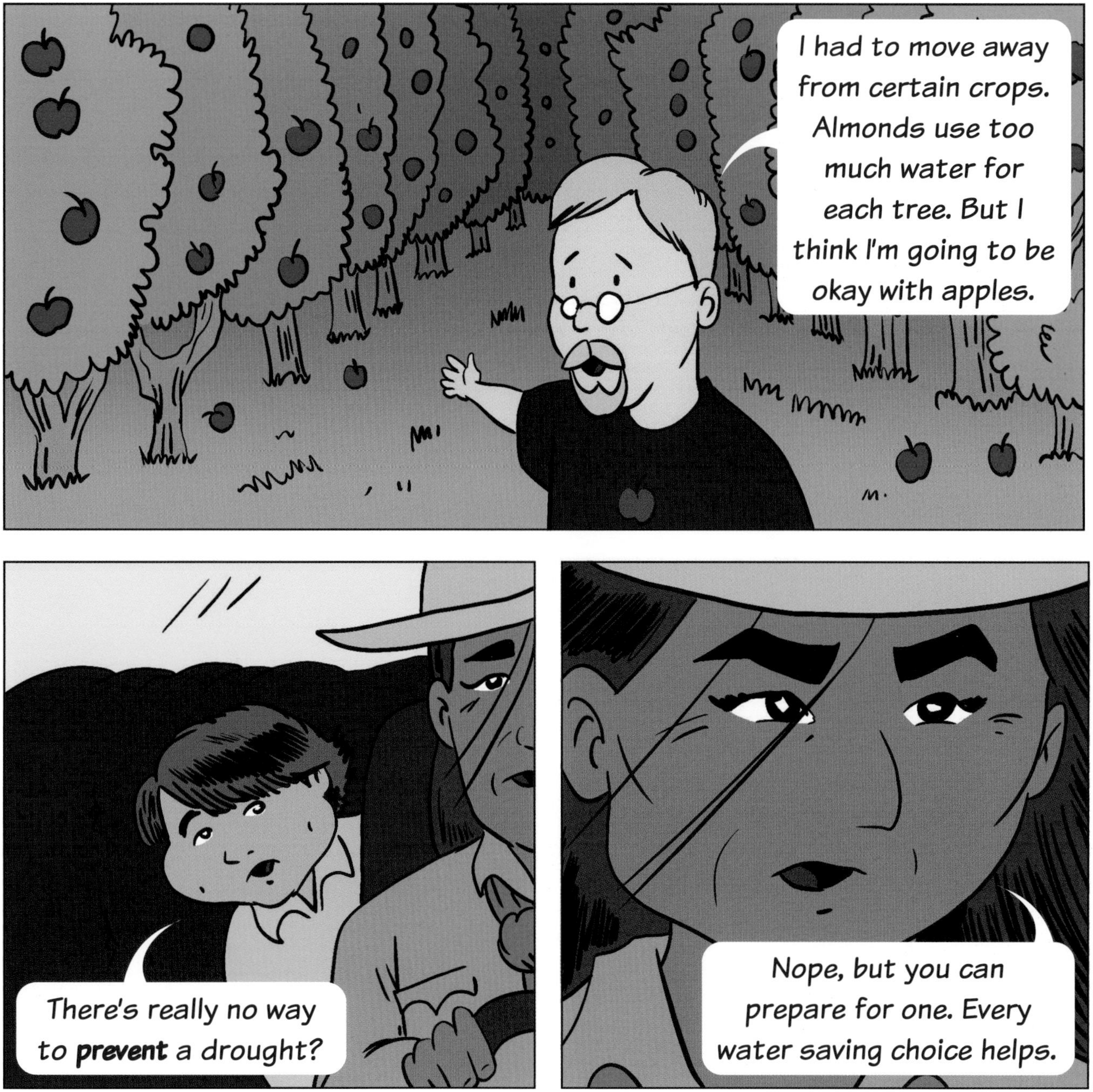
I had to move away from certain crops. Almonds use too much water for each tree. But I think I'm going to be okay with apples.
There's really no way to **prevent** a drought?
Nope, but you can prepare for one. Every water saving choice helps.

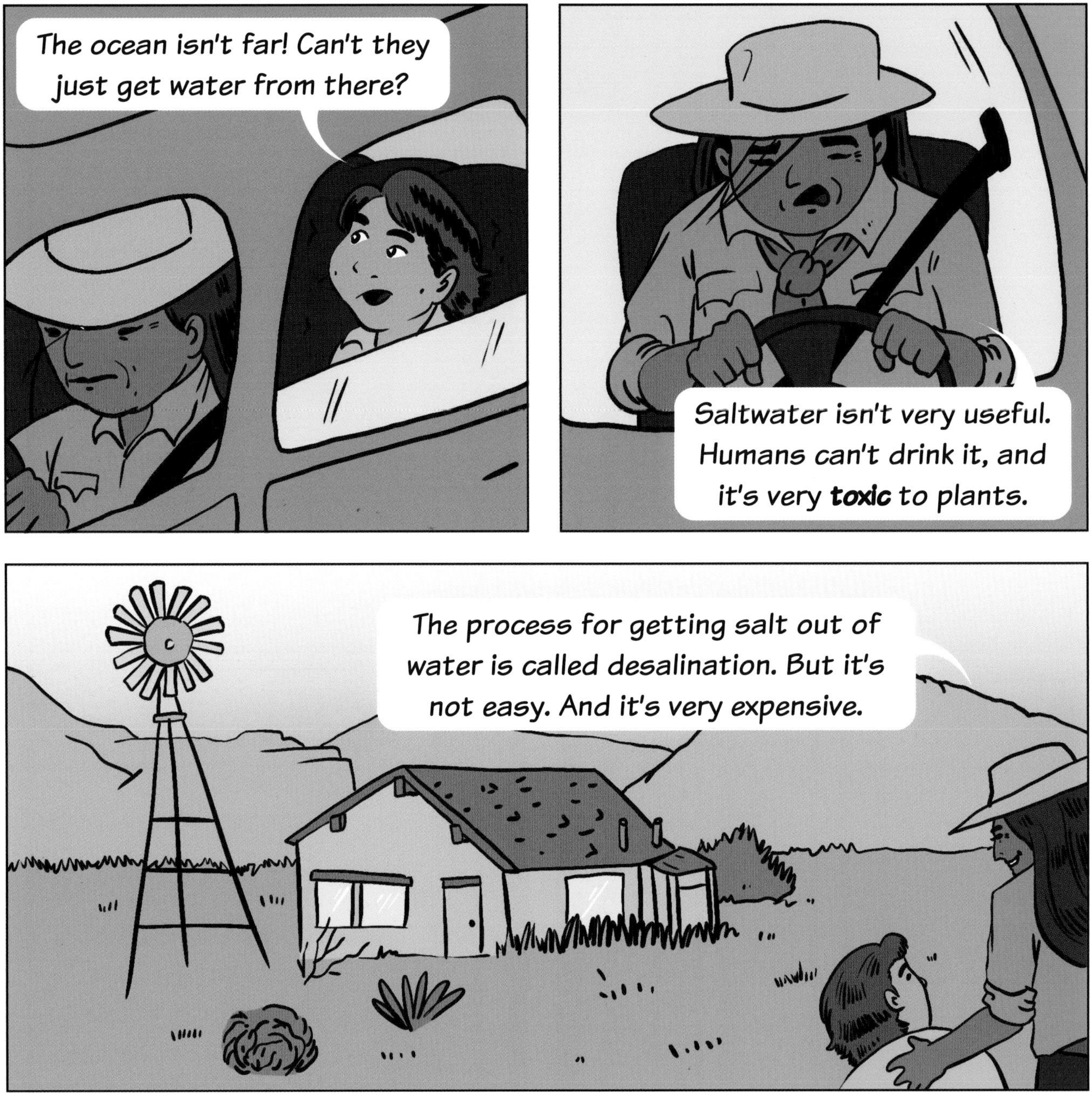
The ocean isn't far! Can't they just get water from there?
Saltwater isn't very useful. Humans can't drink it, and it's very **toxic** to plants.
The process for getting salt out of water is called desalination. But it's not easy. And it's very expensive.

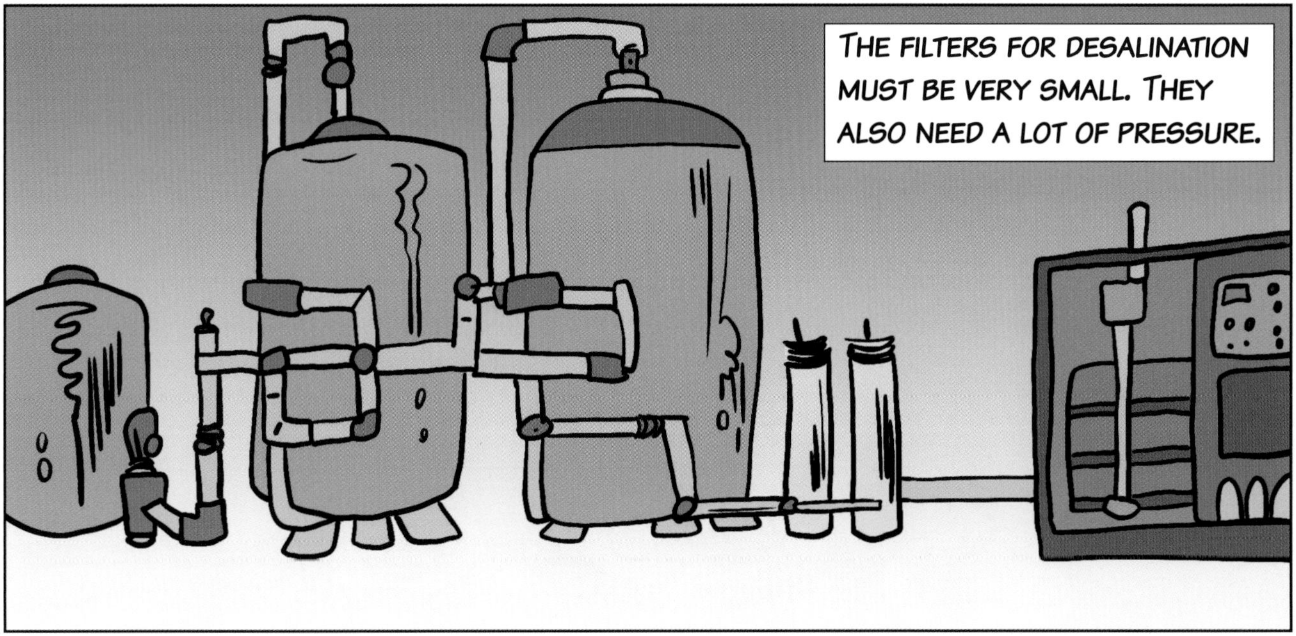
THE FILTERS FOR DESALINATION MUST BE VERY SMALL. THEY ALSO NEED A LOT OF PRESSURE.

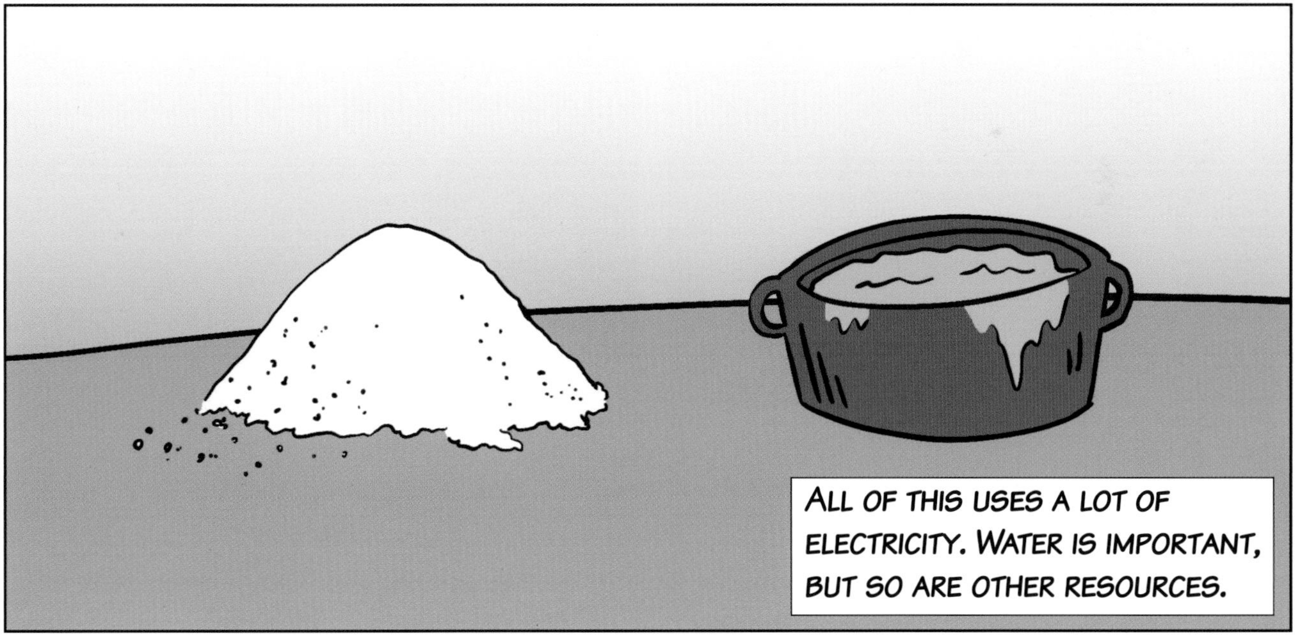
ALL OF THIS USES A LOT OF ELECTRICITY. WATER IS IMPORTANT, BUT SO ARE OTHER RESOURCES.

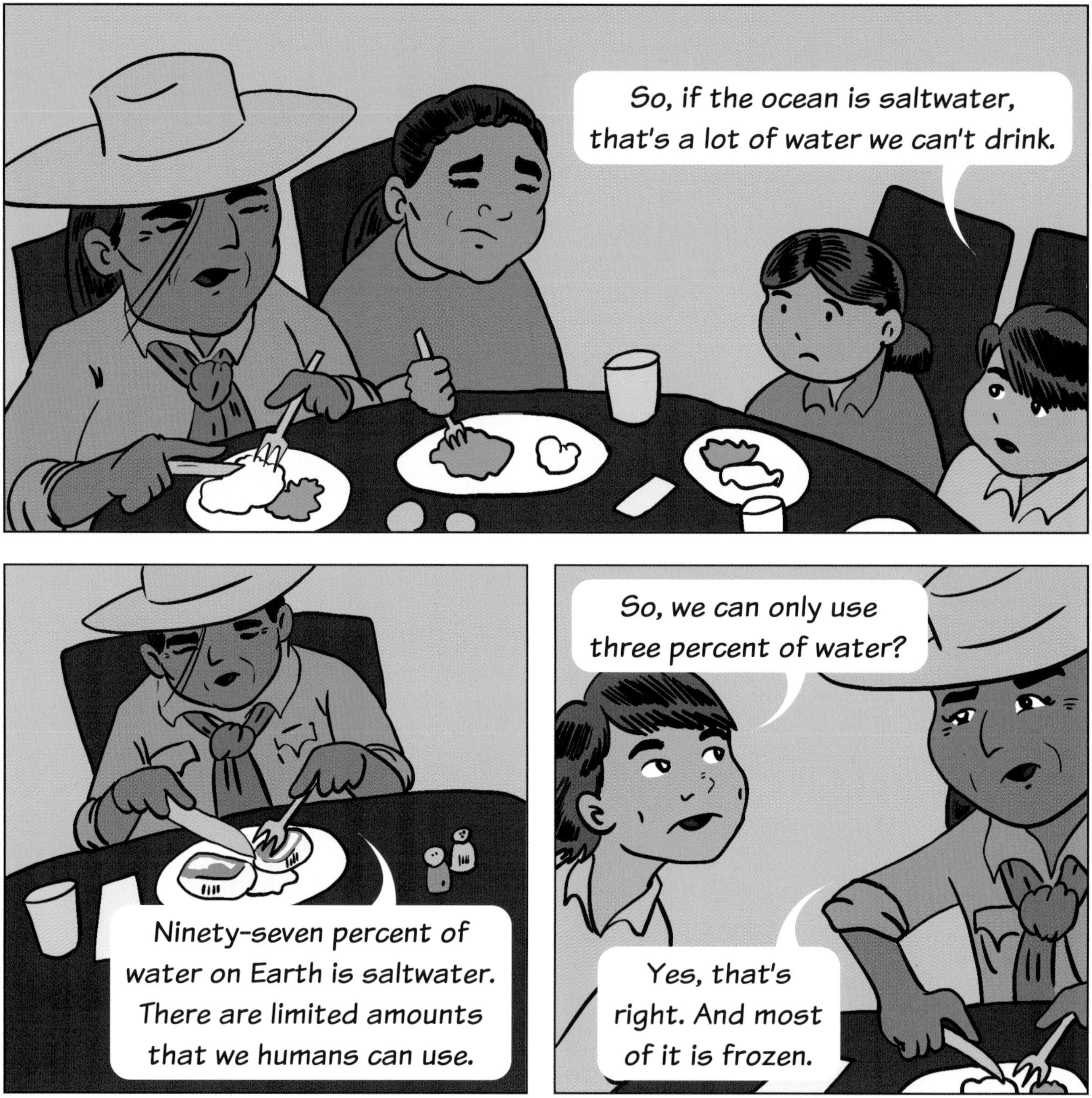
So, if the ocean is saltwater, that's a lot of water we can't drink.
Ninety-seven percent of water on Earth is saltwater. There are limited amounts that we humans can use.
So, we can only use three percent of water?
Yes, that's right. And most of it is frozen.

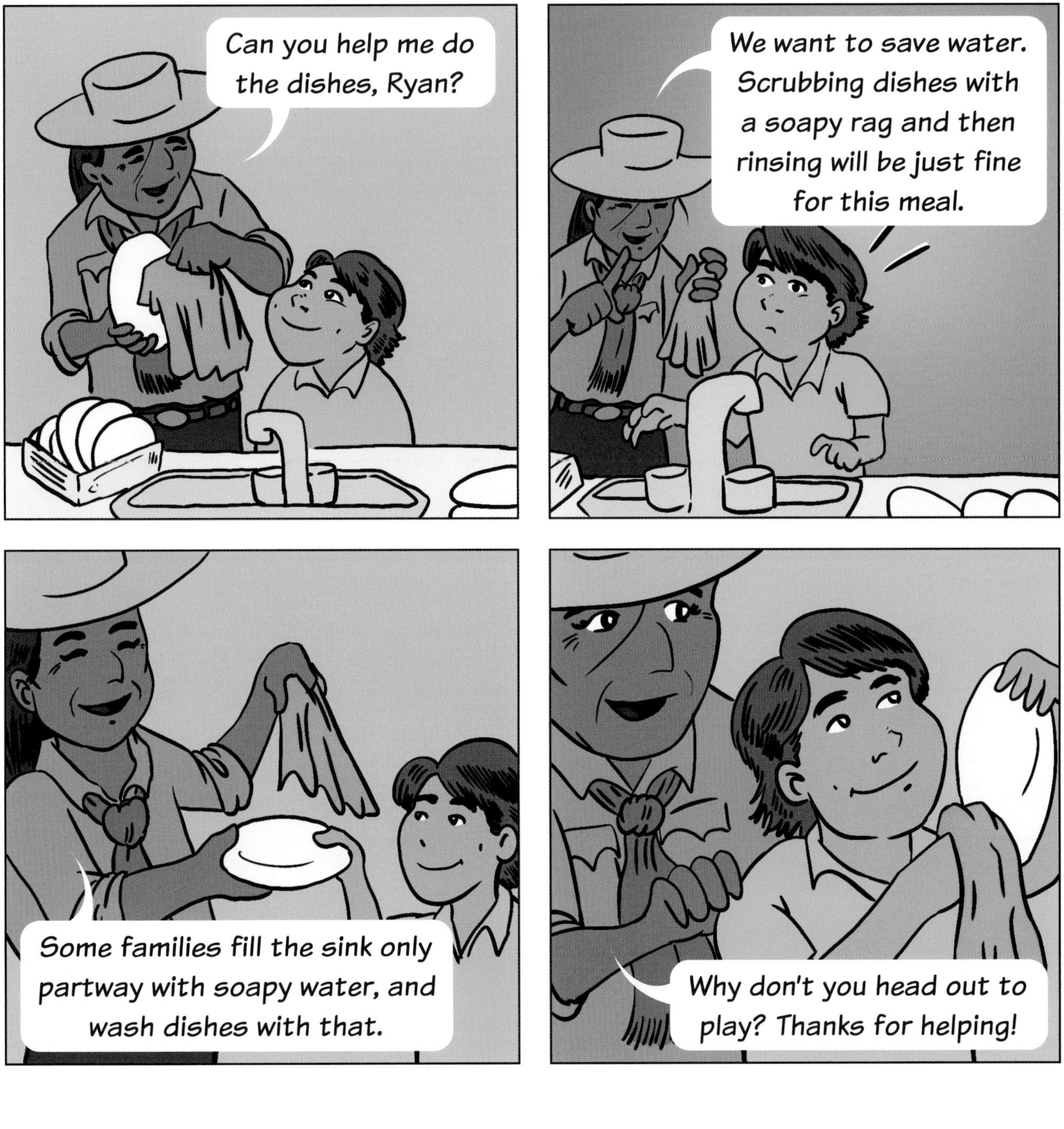
Can you help me do the dishes, Ryan?
We want to save water. Scrubbing dishes with a soapy rag and then rinsing will be just fine for this meal.
Some families fill the sink only partway with soapy water, and wash dishes with that.
Why don't you head out to play? Thanks for helping!

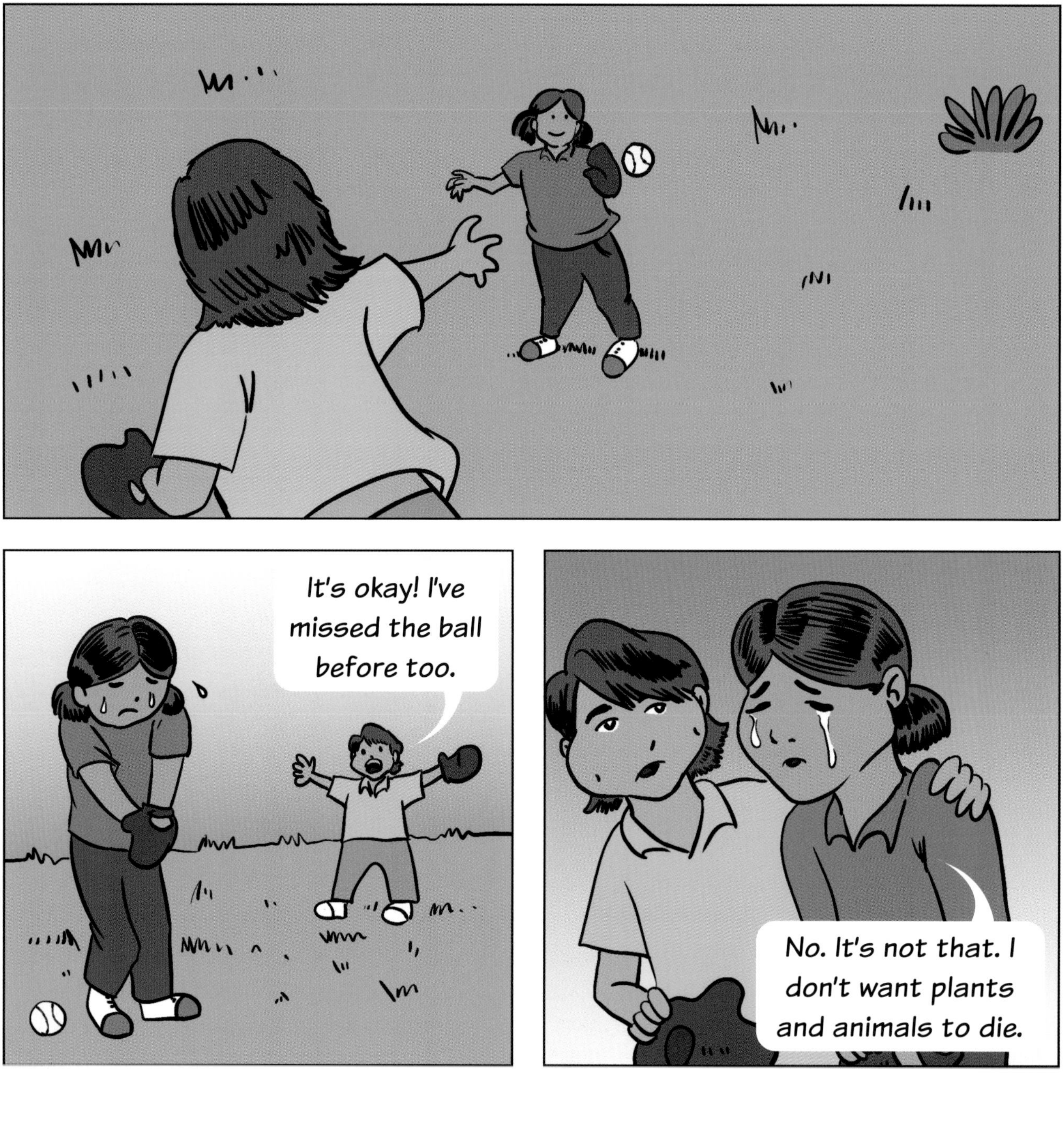
It's okay! I've missed the ball before too.
No. It's not that. I don't want plants and animals to die.

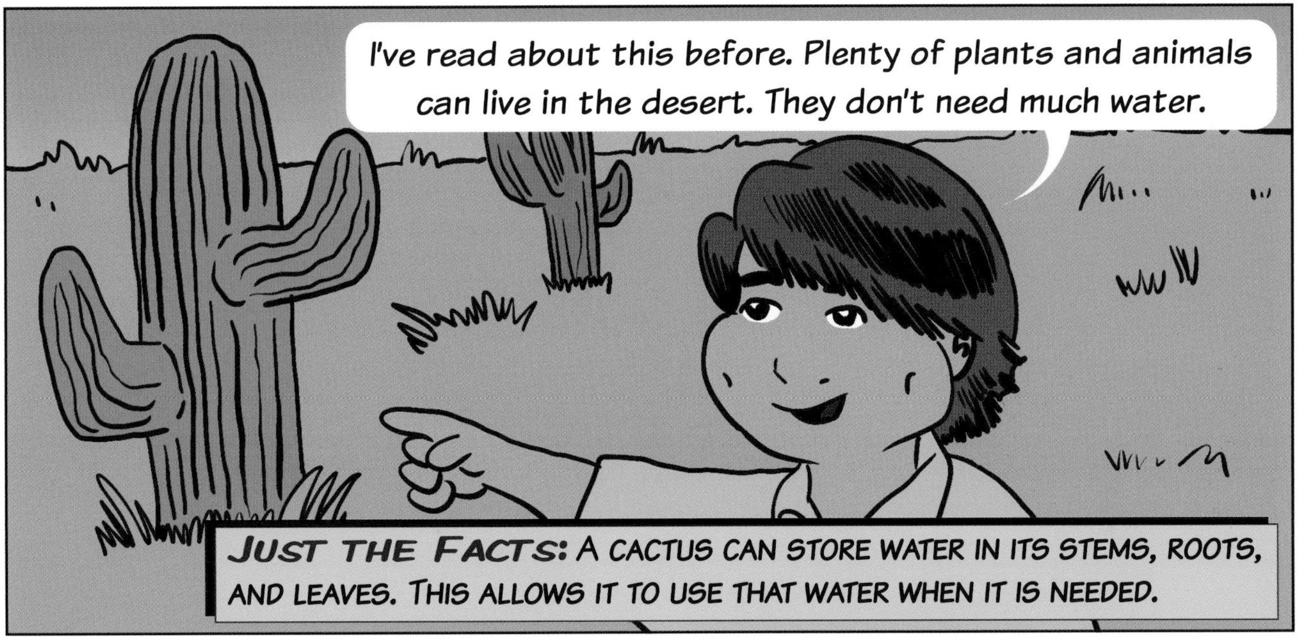
I've read about this before. Plenty of plants and animals can live in the desert. They don't need much water.
JUST THE FACTS: A CACTUS CAN STORE WATER IN ITS STEMS, ROOTS, AND LEAVES. THIS ALLOWS IT TO USE THAT WATER WHEN IT IS NEEDED.

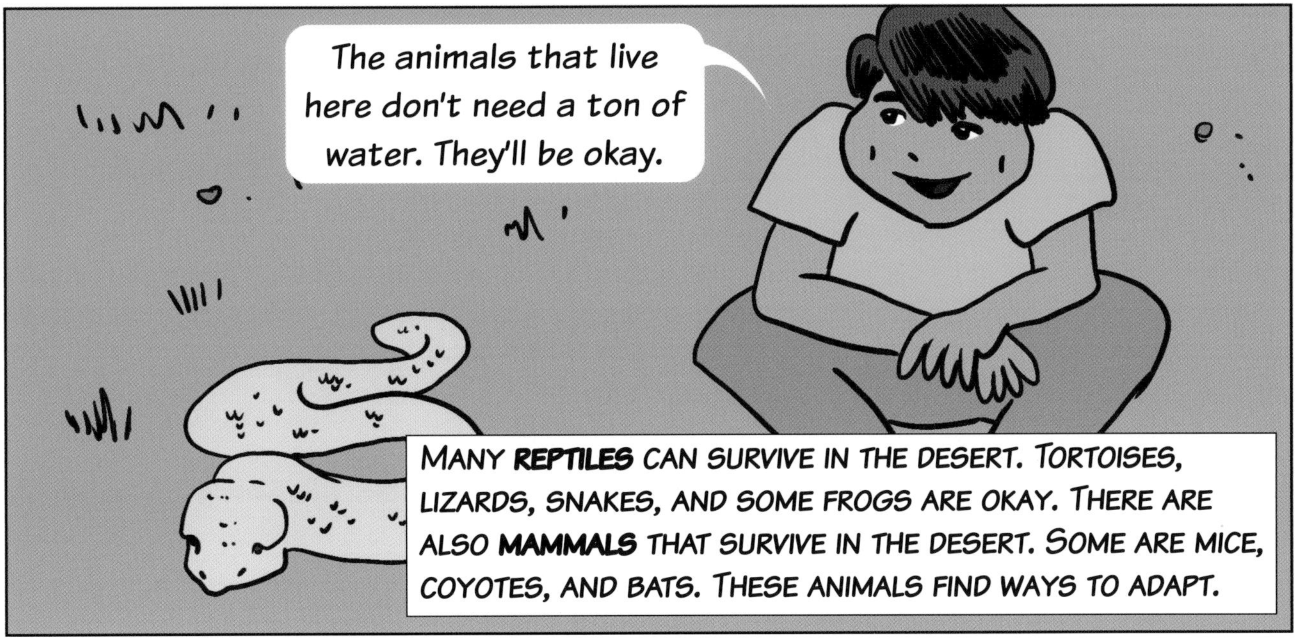
The animals that live here don't need a ton of water. They'll be okay.
MANY **REPTILES** CAN SURVIVE IN THE DESERT. TORTOISES, LIZARDS, SNAKES, AND SOME FROGS ARE OKAY. THERE ARE ALSO **MAMMALS** THAT SURVIVE IN THE DESERT. SOME ARE MICE, COYOTES, AND BATS. THESE ANIMALS FIND WAYS TO ADAPT.

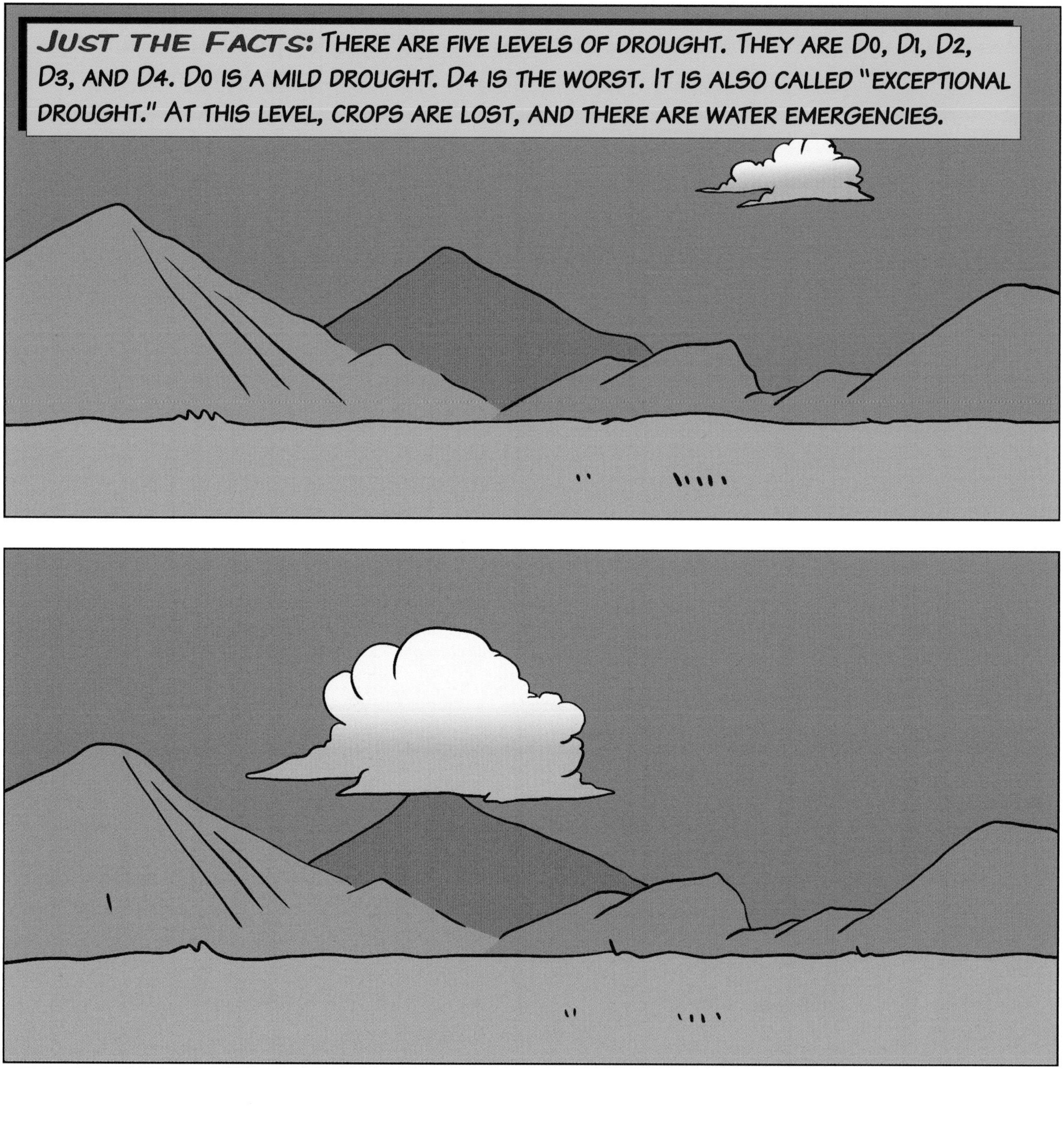
JUST THE FACTS: THERE ARE FIVE LEVELS OF DROUGHT. THEY ARE D0, D1, D2, D3, AND D4. D0 IS A MILD DROUGHT. D4 IS THE WORST. IT IS ALSO CALLED "EXCEPTIONAL DROUGHT." AT THIS LEVEL, CROPS ARE LOST, AND THERE ARE WATER EMERGENCIES.

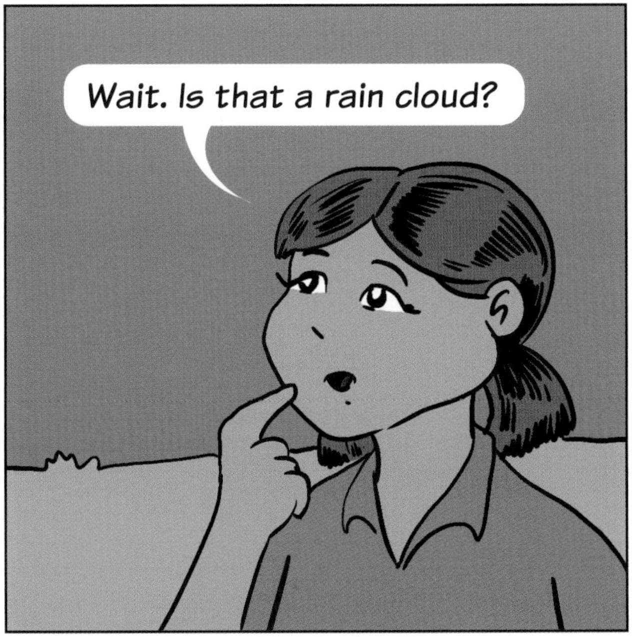
Wait. Is that a rain cloud?

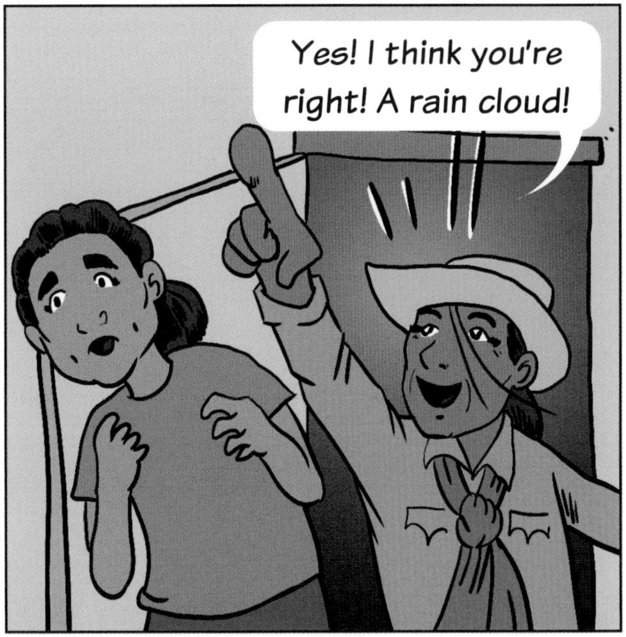
Yes! I think you're right! A rain cloud!

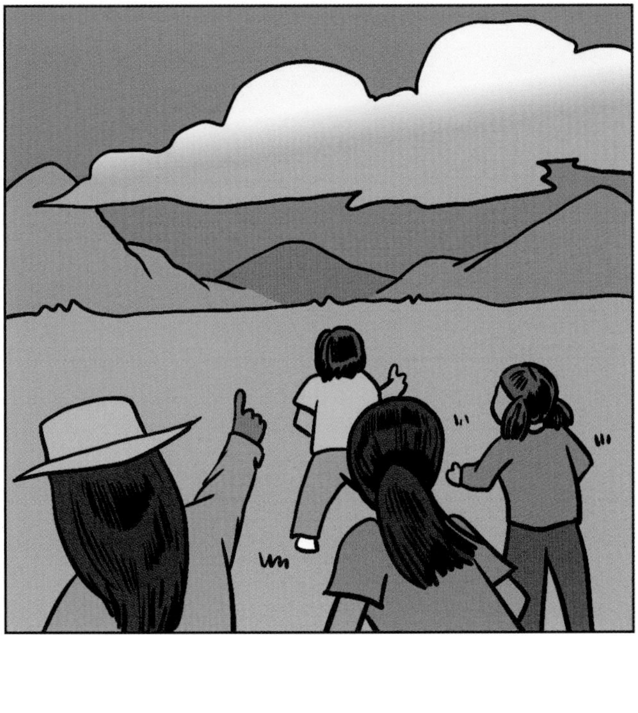

Water Worry

For much of the world, droughts are a major concern. Having access to clean water is important for human life. Globally, 44% of people say they're more scared of a drought than anything else.

I can't believe it... This is real rain!

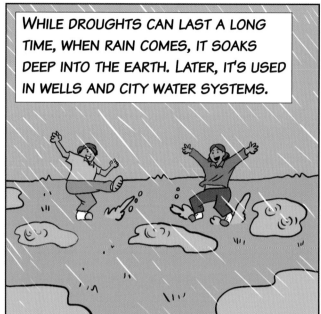

While droughts can last a long time, when rain comes, it soaks deep into the earth. Later, it's used in wells and city water systems.

JUST THE FACTS: Earth's average rainfall per year is about 39 inches (100 cm).

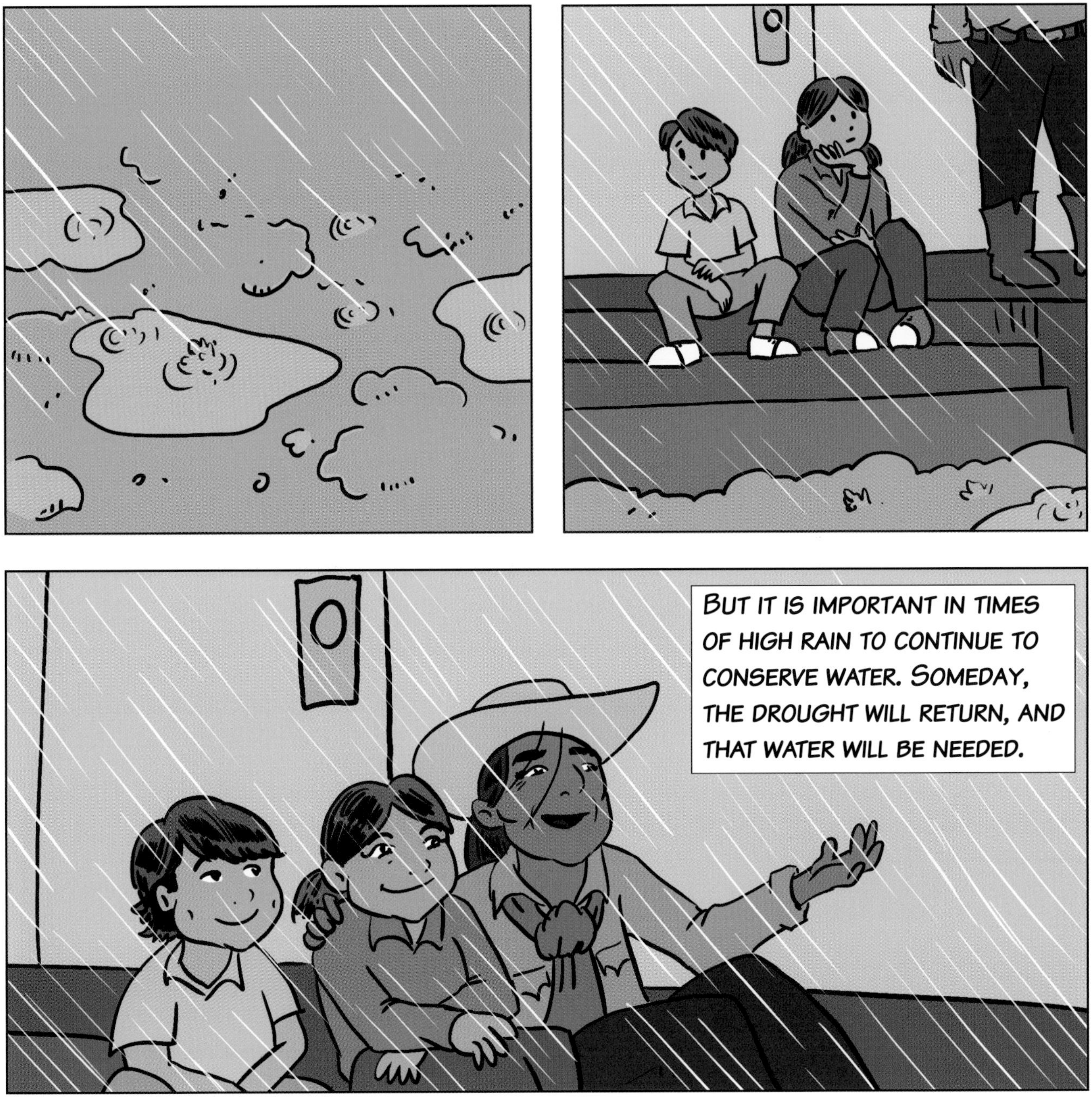
BUT IT IS IMPORTANT IN TIMES OF HIGH RAIN TO CONTINUE TO CONSERVE WATER. SOMEDAY, THE DROUGHT WILL RETURN, AND THAT WATER WILL BE NEEDED.

What to Do About Droughts?

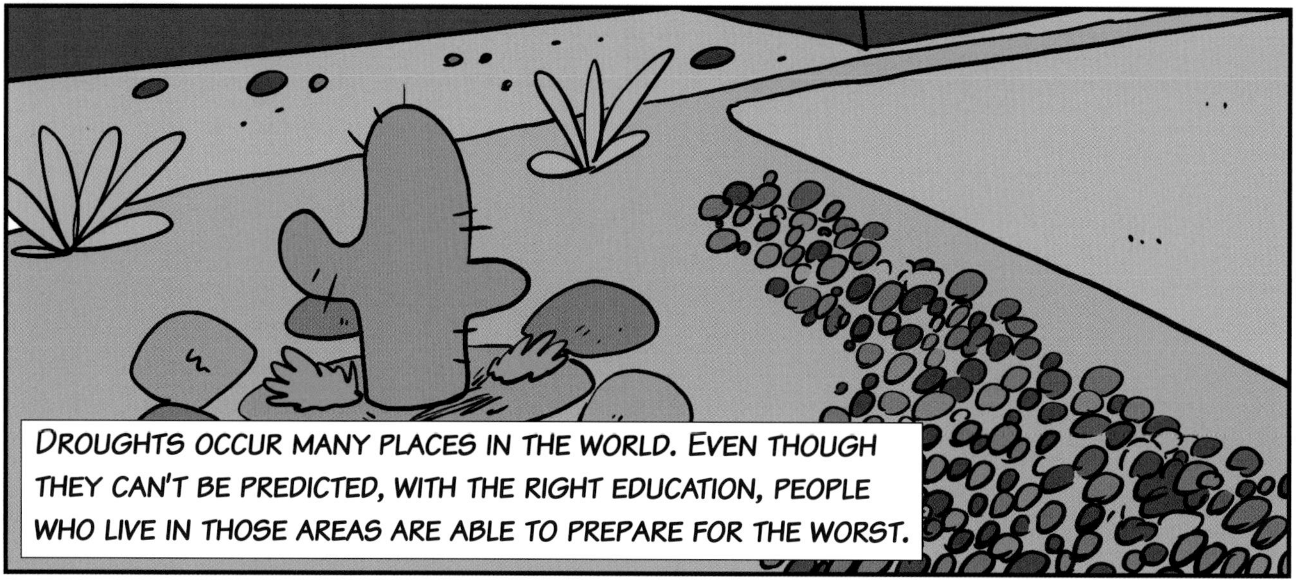
Droughts occur many places in the world. Even though they can't be predicted, with the right education, people who live in those areas are able to prepare for the worst.

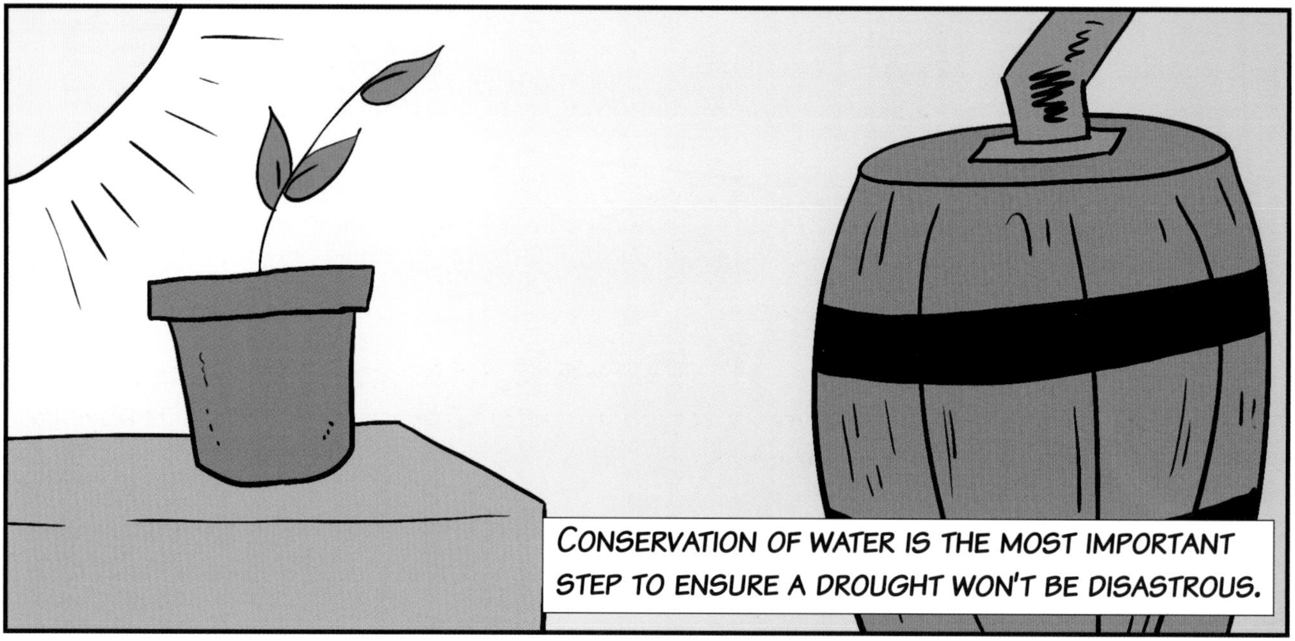
Conservation of water is the most important step to ensure a drought won't be disastrous.

GLOSSARY

atmosphere: the mixture of gases that surrounds the earth

climates: the usual weather patterns and conditions in a particular place over periods of time

condenses: changes from a gas to a liquid

conserving: protecting something from being wasted or lost

evaporates: changes from a liquid to a gas

exceptional: something that is unusual or different from normal

mammals: a warm-blood animal that has hair or fur and gives birth

orchard: an area of land where fruit trees are planted

prevent: to keep from happening

reptiles: a cold-blooded animal with dry scaly skin that lays eggs

restrictions: rules or limitations about what is allowed

toxic: harmful or poisonous

FURTHER READING

Morris, Neil. *Droughts*. Chicago, IL: World Book, Inc., 2018. The characteristics and patterns of droughts, plus descriptions of major droughts that have occurred around the world throughout history.

Rajczak, Michael. *Deadly Droughts* (Where's the Water?). New York: Gareth Stevens Publishing, 2017. This book explores the negative effects of droughts on areas around the world, as well as how particular regions handle droughts when they occur.

Drought For Kids (https://drought.unl.edu/Education/DroughtforKids.aspx) Learn more about the impacts of drought on people's lives and get information from researchers about ways to lessen a drought's damage to the environment.

Weather WizKids: Drought (http://weatherwizkids.com/?page_id=89) Find out more about the different types of droughts and where they are most likely to occur, as well as what to do during drought conditions.

ABOUT THE AUTHOR

Alexander Lowe is a writer who splits his time between Los Angeles and Chicago. He has written children's books about sports, technology, science, and media. He has also done extensive work as a sportswriter and film critic. He loves reading books of any and all kinds.

ABOUT THE ILLUSTRATOR

Sebastian Kadlecik is a screenwriter, actor, and comic book maker. He is best known as the creator of the epic action saga *Penguins vs. Possums*, about a secret, interspecies war for dominion over the earth, and the Eisner-nominated *Quince*, about a young Latina who gets superpowers at her quinceañera.